SPECIAL MESSAGE TO READERS

THE ULVERSCROFT FOUNDATION
(registered UK charity number 264873)
was established in 1972 to provide funds for
research, diagnosis and treatment of eye diseases.
Examples of major projects funded by
the Ulverscroft Foundation are:-

- The Children's Eye Unit at Moorfields Eye Hospital, London
- The Ulverscroft Children's Eye Unit at Great Ormond Street Hospital for Sick Children
- Funding research into eye diseases and treatment at the Department of Ophthalmology, University of Leicester
- The Ulverscroft Vision Research Group, Institute of Child Health
- Twin operating theatres at the Western Ophthalmic Hospital, London
- The Chair of Ophthalmology at the Royal Australian College of Ophthalmologists

You can help further the work of the Foundation
by making a donation or leaving a legacy.
Every contribution is gratefully received. If you
would like to help support the Foundation or
require further information, please contact:

THE ULVERSCROFT FOUNDATION
The Green, Bradgate Road, Anstey
Leicester LE7 7FU, England
Tel: (0116) 236 4325

website: www.foundation.ulverscroft.com

A MAN CALLED BREED

They call him Breed . . . and when he is threatened with violence — because of his Indian heritage — he severely wounds Reed Fowley and seeks refuge in the desert. But Fowley, with his father and brothers, makes sure he's found — locating his homestead in Lone Pine Canyon, below the Mogollon Rim. They hire Robert Candless and a band of savage outlaws to kill him. Now, Breed and Blessing, his wife-to-be, along with his protégé Sparrow, must fight for their lives . . . or die.

Books by Chuck Tyrell
in the Linford Western Library:

VULTURE GOLD
GUNS OF PONDEROSA
THE KILLING TRAIL
HELL FIRE IN PARADISE

CHUCK TYRELL

A MAN
CALLED BREED

Complete and Unabridged

LINFORD
Leicester

First published in Great Britain in 2011 by
Robert Hale Limited
London

First Linford Edition
published 2013
by arrangement with
Robert Hale Limited
London

A catalogue record for this book is available
from the British Library.

ISBN 978–1–4448–1529–0

Published by
F. A. Thorpe (Publishing)
Anstey, Leicestershire

Set by Words & Graphics Ltd.
Anstey, Leicestershire
Printed and bound in Great Britain by
T. J. International Ltd., Padstow, Cornwall

This book is printed on acid-free paper

For Yukiko, a Blessing to me

1

I lay at the edge of a ridge overlooking Adam's Well, watching. I'd come a far way from Ehrenburg on the Colorado River and the well held the only water in twenty miles. Zeeb, my brindle grulla, smelled the water and tossed his head, rustling the leaves of the scrub-oak thicket where he stood.

Below, a faded yellow wagon sat by the rock-bound pool. The horses were out of the traces and cropping at the sparse grama grass. I took my time. I had to see what kind of people were at the well before me.

The sound of a hard female voice drifted up. 'Get your cracker ass moving.'

A red-headed woman in a tight-waisted low-cut gingham dress strode to a dark-haired one who was washing clothes in a tub at the edge of the pool.

She swung a roundhouse at the smaller woman. A moment later the smack reached my ears, accompanied by a squeak. The little one looked like a kid.

I took a long look at the man. Back against a willow tree, spraddle-legged, hat over his eyes, he didn't move. Either he slept sound or he was ignoring the woman.

'I want clean bloomers, bitch,' the woman said.

'It'll only take a little while, Miss Polly, just a minute,' the girl pleaded. 'The water's clear and good, and I got a bit of soap. Only a minute more. Honest.'

The whore — I decided Polly was a very soiled dove; nothing else could make a woman so hard — flounced to a wooden chair over by the wagon and sat. 'Just you get along with it. That's all I've got to say.' Polly bit at a fingernail, then rubbed her palms along her thighs. She heaved a sigh, scratched one armpit, then the other. She jumped up and climbed the steps at the rear of the wagon. A moment later, she reappeared with a silk Chinese fan in her hand. 'I hate Arizona,' she said. 'Hot as hell. Maybe hotter.'

The girl rinsed indigo bloomers and white cotton chemises, wrung the water from them, and spread them on a nearby manzanita bush to dry. 'All done, Miss Polly,' she announced.

Polly rose and stalked over to inspect the laundry. She reached a hand to the girl's face and gave her left cheek a twisting pinch. 'Someday you'll be decent help,' she said, 'if Garfield don't sell you to the Mexicans first.'

The girl put a hand to her face, but stood still, her head bowed.

No spirit left, I figured. Still, I saw nothing alarming about the trio, but decided to keep an eye on the sleeper. I scuttled back from the lip of the ridge, mounted Zeeb, and worked my way down the front side of the slope toward Adam's Well.

The trio at the wagon looked like greenhorns. None of them noticed me

3

until Zeeb was at the bottom of the ridge.

'Garfield. Garfield! There's a guy on a horse coming this way.' The whore's voice rose an octave, like she'd concluded I might be dangerous.

I ignored the man and his two women, and rode Zeeb to the edge of the well. The girl backed away from the water, her hands at her mouth and her eyes wide.

Polly watched, her legs spread like she was inviting me.

Garfield didn't move.

Faded letters on the wagon side read PLEASURE PALACE. I should have guessed. A whorehouse on wheels. I turned Zeeb and stepped out of the saddle with him between me and the wagon people.

'Looking for a good time?' Polly the whore simpered.

'Not the kind you'd give,' I said. 'Not in a hurry to catch the clap ... or worse.'

Polly pouted.

'My girls have no diseases.'

'Garfield! Such language.' Then Polly giggled.

'Invite our visitor to dinner, Polly. The sun will soon be down, and there's no need for him to ride on while food and water and certain entertainments are available here.' Garfield removed his hat, brushed a lion's mane of tawny hair back over his head, and clamped the bowler down over it.

'Mister?' Polly's voice was tentative. 'You can stay for dinner if you want.'

'I reckon jackrabbit and prickly pears'd be better'n anything you all could cook,' I said. 'I'll be moving on.' I knelt by the pool and scooped some of the clear water into my mouth. It smelled of granite and tasted wet, not muddy like a lot of desert water. Zeeb stood between me and the wagon people like he was on guard. I filled two canteens and hung them by their straps over the saddle horn.

'Mister?' The girl moved a little closer around the edge of the pool.

I ignored her and urged Zeeb to take another drink, then fitted him with a gunnysack nosebag. The only sounds were Zeeb munching dry oats and the girl's breathing.

'Mister?'

I looked at her.

'I'll cook real good.' The girl's voice pleaded and so did her eyes. 'Can't you stay for dinner?'

'You cooking?'

She nodded. 'I always do.'

I turned away and stared at the pool for a long moment, then looked up. 'I'll stay if you want, but there are men on my back trail . . . men who'll shoot first and ask for explanations later.' I didn't mention the canvas money-belt under my union suit, filled with half a hundred gold double eagles earned with hard work and cunning and an ability to train horses well, coins from the sale of forty-nine prime mustangs to the quartermaster at Fort Yuma.

'We got beans and some chilli peppers. I can make fry bread, too.' The girl's voice got stronger.

I grubbed through my saddlebags and pulled out a fist-sized lump wrapped in a piece of flour-sack cloth. 'Half a rabbit,' I said. 'Can't have no *chili con carne* without it's got meat in it.' I held out the lump to the girl.

Her eyes went wide. 'Meat?' She took a hesitant step toward me. 'Can I use it? Really?'

I nodded, still holding the lump out toward her.

'Take the meat, damn it.' Garfield's voice had a hard edge to it.

The girl shrank back into herself. She kept her eyes on the ground as she came up to me.

I studied her as she approached. Thin. Too thin. Dark complexion, but not Mex. Simple cotton dress. Likely nothing underneath. She barely came to my shoulder.

She took the meat. 'Thank you, sir,' she said. 'My name is Blessing.' She stood there, waiting to hear my name.

'I'm just passing through, Blessing,' I

said. 'My name don't matter. Leave it be.'

Blessing reached out to pat Zeeb. 'Your horse sure looks funny, mister,' she said.

Zeeb snuffled at her dress and decided he didn't mind the young woman.

'Zeeb's taken a liking to you, Blessing. You must be something special.' I smiled.

Blessing blushed. 'Thank you for the meat, mister. I'll surely make *chili con carne y frijoles*. The beans is already done.' She returned to the wagon, put the meat away, picked up a hand axe, and went out in the brush. Probably looking for firewood. A jay chattered in the alders back of the pool. The other two could have been hunks of stone for all they moved.

I took the saddle off Zeeb and turned him loose to graze. The brindle grulla was as good as a watchdog, and he'd come whenever I whistled.

Blessing came back through the

brush with an armload of sticks.

'You build the fire,' I said. 'I'll get more wood.'

'You don't have to do that. You being a guest and all.'

I smiled again. 'My mother always said I should do my share. Wouldn't want to disappoint her.' I took her hand axe and walked out into the desert.

Adam's Well lies in the foothills on the western slope of the Kofa Mountains, overlooking the basin that stretches across more than forty miles of desert to the Trigo range. On the other side of the Trigoes, Ehrenburg squats on the eastern bank of the Colorado River, scraping out a living from the steamboats that paddle north and south from the Sea of Cortez to the point where the shallows start at La Paz.

A week ago, Zeeb and I took a river steamer north from Arizona City and landed in Ehrenburg. The trip gave Zeeb some time to rest and I got in a bit of gambling with a would-be shark. His teeth weren't long enough, and my dark poker-face let me bluff him out of nigh on $400. A decent grubstake that meant I could leave the gold in my money belt — double eagles to buy land and good horses to graze the long grass along Cherry Creek in the Tonto Basin.

If I'd just stayed out of the Black Diamond, I could have ridden straight for Cherry Creek instead of looping through the desert. But that's not how things work for the likes of me.

The Black Diamond didn't even have batwings. Just a plain white door that opened to a long skinny room with a bar down the left-hand wall and a row of five tables to the right.

I'm not one to wear a sixgun. I prefer a Bowie up close and a one-in-a-thousand Winchester '73 when there's room. Folks talk about fast guns, but no gunman can get his iron out faster than I can shuck a Bowie. Up close, cold steel's best.

When I opened the door, three of the five men in the saloon turned to size me up. I knew what they saw. A man too dark to be all white. A man who wore knee-high Apache moccasins and had a fourteen-inch Bowie aslant his left hip with its grip close to hand. A man in faded Levis and canvas shirt with longish black hair curling out from under a battered Stetson. A man with a Winchester '73. I wasn't a pretty sight.

'Turley's Mill?' I said to the barkeep. I leaned the rifle against the bar, muzzle up.

He shook his head. 'Old Potrero out of San Francisco's the best I've got.'

'Gimme.'

'Dollar a shot. I see the dollar, I pour the whiskey.'

I put a cartwheel on the bar. 'Trusting soul, eh?'

The 'keep gave me a curl of the lip that may have been a smile. He took the silver dollar and poured a finger of amber into a cloudy glass. He pushed the drink across the bar in my direction. 'Was I you, I'd make that my last drink,' he said.

I gave him a broad smile. 'I'm just getting started.' I tossed the whiskey and thumped the empty glass on the bar. ' 'Nother,' I said, and dug in my pocket for a second silver dollar.

The door swung open to let a big chunky man walk in. Although young, his gait was ponderous. He planted each foot like his legs were stone columns. His face, thrust forward, was covered with three-day stubble and an unfriendly scowl. He stopped two steps away and shucked his gun.

'You.' The voice sounded like a rumble deep in some distant cave.

'Me?' I shifted to face the man.

'Yeah. You. Git.'

I smiled and kept my body loose. 'I just put a dollar on the bar,' I said, my tone as reasonable as I could make it.

'Your kind don't belong with regular folks. Git.'

'Reckon my cash is the same color as yours,' I said with my best poker face. 'I've got another dollar. Buy you a drink. This Old Potrero ain't bad

12

booze.' I waved at the bar. 'How 'bout it?' I didn't really want to tangle with the big man, but I wouldn't back down either, not on account of my skin color, anyway.

He spit on the floor and moved closer. 'Git. Or they'll carry you out.'

I turned my back to him. Slowly. Deliberately. 'Pour that whiskey, bar man,' I said. 'Now.' I pushed the silver dollar at him.

He stood stock still, eyes darting from me to the big man behind me.

A click came as the big man thumbed back the hammer of his .45. I whirled to my right, snaking out my Bowie and slashing through his bicep with its fourteen-inch blade as I turned. My left fist smashed into his square jaw as my momentum carried me past. The .45 clattered to the floor.

The big guy fell to his knees, clutching his half-severed arm with his big left hand. 'You miserable sumbitch.' He mumbled the words. 'Sumbitch. You. Cut. Me!' Blood pumped down

13

his arm to drip off his splayed fingers.

'Feel lucky I didn't cut your miserable throat,' I said. 'Get that bound up,' I said to the 'keep, 'or he'll bleed out.' I picked up the bar towel and wiped the Bowie's blade clean. 'Keep the extra dollar. I was just leaving.' The Winchester came natural to my hand, and I jacked a cartridge into its chamber.

It seemed an awful long way to the door, but I forced myself to walk normal, not too fast, not too slow, the rifle under my arm.

As I neared the door, the barkeep called out. 'Reed Fowley's got family,' he said. 'They'll be wanting to know who done this to their brother and son. What should they call you?'

I stopped with a hand on the door. 'Same as everyone else,' I said. 'They can call me Breed.'

2

I'd not killed big Reed Fowley in Ehrenburg, but the barkeep mentioned family and I had no wish to tangle with a covey of gunmen in their own town. Zeeb carried the necessities: coffee, water, oats . . . The land gave me whatever else I needed. So I stepped out of the Black Diamond and into my saddle. Zeeb could run long and hard if it came to that, but going out of Ehrenburg, we took it easy.

We'd held to the stage road past the Trigoes, then ducked into the desert and headed for Gila Bend. By sundown, dust on my backtrail told me the Fowleys were coming. Until then, I'd ridden natural, not trying to hide any sign of my passing. But with those men after me, I decided it was time to do different.

The first thing I did after spying

those riders was dig into my offside saddlebag for two pairs of rawhide boots that fit Zeeb's shod hoofs. When we rode away from the high point where I'd watched for pursuit, the hoofprints were of an unshod Indian pony, not a whiteman's iron-clad horse. If the Fowleys were any good, they'd figure out what I'd done. Then I'd have to do something more drastic.

Late in the evening I spotted a barrel cactus. Zeeb was mountain born and desert bred. He'd eat anything that didn't wear feathers or fur. I lopped the top off the cactus with my Bowie and cut its heart out. Part I fed to Zeeb. The moisture in the pulp would keep him going. Part I squeezed in my fist and lapped the juice as it ran down the heel of my hand. It tasted like deserts smell, but it was wet and would keep me alive unless someone's bullet put out the spark.

That night I didn't eat. I saw rabbits and ground squirrels and coveys of quail, but didn't want to let the Fowleys know where I was by using my rifle to feed myself. I'd pick some prickly pears in the morning and eat while I watched the backtrail. If no one showed, I'd head for Eagle Tanks. If those hard men were still out there, I'd do something to discourage them.

I slept rolled in the saddle blanket. Night in the desert can turn cold.

Zeeb got another mess of barrel cactus pulp for breakfast. He acted like it suited him just fine.

The sun rose over my back as I lay on an outcropping. No matter how good a tracker is, he can't see in the dark. The Fowleys shouldn't have gained any time on me, but somehow they did.

A whiffle of dust rose in the slanting rays of the sun and, beneath the dust, four horsemen; one out front by fifty yards or so. The Fowleys had a tracker, and he was no tenderfoot. I carried a pair of field glasses I'd relieved from Army service when I worked as a civilian scout, and they came in handy at times like this. The sun was at my back so there was little chance of reflection giving away my position. I fished the field glasses from their pouch and focused on the dust plume.

The man in the lead rode with his head down, eyes on my trail. The three behind wore Stetsons, cowhide vests, and shotgun chaps, looking like cowboys but with none of the cowboy slouch in the way they rode their horses. The loose clothing, bandanna headband, and shoulder-length hair of the leading rider told me he was Indian, probably Pima. He was the reason the Fowleys had gained on me during the night.

Killing doesn't set well with me, although the men who rode after me probably had murder on their minds. All three carried rifles balanced across their saddle bows. The Indian rode with a trapdoor Springfield in the crook of his arm and a bandolier of 45–90 shells over his shoulder. Through my field glasses, the Springfield looked well cared for, unlike the arms many Indians bore. He'd had army training at the least and may have been one of the barefoot legion of Mexes and Pimas that fought in the war. I hoped to steer shy of that man. Still, I had to discourage the Fowleys. I decided to do it head on.

I chose a rock formation that poked out of the desert floor like a set of giant fingers. Earlier, Zeeb and I had kept it to our right as we went by, then doubled back. Sooner or later, the Fowley party would come this way. I settled down to wait.

Sounds of a horse walking reached me before I saw the scout. He worked his mount carefully, clearly aware that the rocks made a good place for an ambush. I sat still as the stones around me, not even blinking. I kept my eyes on a spot I imagined was a dozen feet above the Pima. Then I recognized him. John Walker. A half-breed, like me, who'd married a Pima and had adopted her people's ways. He'd been an officer of the Arizona Volunteers, a regiment of

Pima and Maricopa Indians with a few whites and Mexicans mixed in. People said Walker could track lizards across bare rock.

'Walker?' I pitched my voice low so it reached his ears and no further.

He reined in his buckskin. I know horses, and Walker's was one of the best I'd seen in a long time.

'Walker?' I said again.

He gave a slight nod that a body might not notice if he weren't looking for it.

'Reed Fowley pulled a gun on me. Cocked the hammer. Threatened me. All because my mother is Cheyenne. I didn't kill him. So why are his people chasing me?'

Walker edged the buckskin closer to the rocks. 'Yudisthir,' he said, using the name the Apaches gave me. 'I know of you. None are better in the desert, except myself, perhaps. What would you do?'

'I want to talk to the Fowleys without them seeing me. I prefer not to kill, but

I will if I must.'

Again Walker gave me a slight nod. He turned the buckskin back the way he'd come, and soon I heard horses walking my way.

'Fowley!' I hollered. I was out of sight and the rocks would scatter my voice, making it hard for the Fowleys to pinpoint my position.

The horses stopped, but the riders said nothing.

'Fowley!'

'I'll be Sean Fowley,' a solid voice with an Irish brogue said. 'Ya cut me son. Ya'll pay.'

'Your son held a Colt's revolver at my back, Fowley. Was I Johnny Ringo, he'd be dead.'

'Ya ain't nothing but a 'breed. 'Breed's got no right to cut me boy.'

'Sean Fowley. Hear me. I could have cut Reed Fowley's throat as easily as I cut his arm, but I don't hold to killing people. I'll go a long way to keep from having to kill a man, but I've got my limits.'

A whoop of laughter came from where the horses were stopped. 'Hey, 'breed. My name's Bud Fowley, and me and my brother Thad, well, we're just plain gonna slit your throat . . . or maybe hang you, 'breed bastard, that's all there is to it.'

'Fowleys! All of you. Hear me, and hear me good. I was just passing through your town, not even gonna spend the night, but your brainless brother took it into his head to run me out. I don't run worth a damn.'

The third man spoke. ' 'Breeds gotta stay with they own kind. You drunk at the cantina in Mex town, you'd live. Now you'll die.' The words were brave, but the voice was a bit shaky.

'John Walker,' I called.

I heard a grunt.

'You know of me, Walker. The desert is my friend. Take those who pay you back to Ehrenburg. I will not kill them, but if they follow me, soon they will wish to die.'

'Shut up, 'breed,' the old man said.

'John Walker's the best. Ye have no kind of edge. Ye'll hang. I swear it.'

I slipped from the rock formation on soundless feet. They'd wait for me to answer, and that would give me enough time to get Zeeb away and into the maze of arroyos that slice up the desert of the Mojave.

By noon I was behind a ridge overlooking my trail. Half a mile away, the Fowleys sat their horses in the harsh sunlight, big men who rode uneasy in their saddles. Walker worked to decipher the confused sign I'd laid for him to follow.

I studied Reed Fowley's kin. The old man Sean sat stolid in his saddle, both hands on the horn. His chin was on his chest and he seemed deep in thought. I slipped my one-in-a-thousand Winchester out onto the ledge in front of me. At 800 yards, I could knock the head off a prairie dog. Right now, I was aiming at something else.

Sooner or later, it had to happen.

Although the two sons looked different — one big, thick, and powerful, like the one I'd cut, the other was slim and wiry. I didn't know who was Thad and who was Bud. Not that it mattered.

When the thickset son lifted his canteen to take a drink in the desert heat, the sights of my Winchester were on it. I gently touched off a shot and watched the canteen fly from his hand, holed and pouring out its precious water on the thirsty ground.

As I slipped away, I heard a faint shout, but I didn't stick around to watch. Smoke from the rifle would tell them where I'd been, and John Walker would have a new place to start tracking from.

Considering what I'd heard of John Walker, I couldn't figure out why he worked for the Fowleys. He'd been a stand-up officer of a volunteer battalion that had a much better record against Apache raiders than any regular army outfit. Didn't seem right, him helping a bunch of townies over a half-breed,

24

especially with himself preferring life with his Pima relatives rather than with white men.

Zeeb and I existed on barrel cactus pulp whenever we found one. By the third day, the Fowleys began to lag and, just before sundown, my field glasses picked them out on the slopes of the Muggins range. They weren't on my trail. Walker was leading them to Tinajas Altos, tanks high in the Muggins mountains. Now I could follow them.

Tinajas Altos were basins worn into the rocks of the Muggins. Because they're deep and high off the desert floor, the run-off they caught from the few rainstorms that came through tended to last longer than the water in shallower tanks. Still, there was no guarantee of water at the Tinajas Altas. I reckoned it was a gamble on John Walker's part.

The Fowleys got there first, which made no nevermind to me. The darkness covered my approach and my

Cheyenne blood and upbringing let me move in without a sound.

Walker had done right. The camp lay some distance from the tanks, so the wild creatures that used the water at night could do so without fear.

I lay on the upside of the hill from Tinajas Altos, searching the surrounds of the camp through my glasses. Even though I looked at every foot of the terrain, it still took me the better part of an hour to spot the man on watch.

He sat in the shadow of a granite spire, protected by a loose ring of boulders, about a hundred yards uphill of the camp. The sentry had a clear field of fire to just about anything he could see. Only I was uphill of him, and out of his line of sight.

I thought to steal one or two of the Fowleys' horses. Losing a horse would make no difference to a desert man like John Walker, but I sized up the Fowleys as townsmen. Tough they were, but only in their own town. Without a mount, John Walker would make his way out of the desert on foot, most likely quicker than if he was riding. To the Fowleys, though, loss of a horse or two would be a big thing.

I snaked around until I found a spot where I could look down on the guard. The skinny Fowley sat in the nest of rocks. He looked dead tired. His head drooped. I figured another hour would see him asleep in his rock nest.

John Walker would watch in the hours before dawn. That's what I'd do — that's what he'd do. I'd have to rustle the horses in the next hour or so.

The horses stood picketed on a sparse patch of grama grass downhill from the camp. The mere fact they were picketed told me they likely didn't belong to the Fowleys. John Walker slept off to one side, leather strap leading from his wrist to his two-color paint. Disturb the horse, disturb the man. Walker didn't live with the Pimas for nothing.

An hour to circle the camp and get downhill of the three Fowley horses. If I got it right and the horses were livery plugs, they'd not be disturbed by a human among them. I crept closer. The horses ignored me.

Walker chose a swale for the camp. It kept the fire out of casual view, but also put the picketed horses below the sightline of the men sleeping by the coals. Walker lay up near the edge of the swale, his head sheltered by a jutting rock. His horse cropped at the chamise, then raised its head to watch while it chewed. The sound of the horse's chomping covered the tiny sounds of my progress toward the picketed ponies, but his ears pricked in my direction. Apparently Walker's horse decided I was benign because he never broke his crop-and-chew rhythm.

I decided to steal two ponies. A man can handle one horse on a lead line all right, but two can be a problem when the cayuses are on the run. I slipped between a dark sorrel and a white-legged black. They turned their heads to sniff at me. They found me no different from the scores of humans that walked in and out of their equine lives.

The livery mounts wore halters with the picket lines attached. I cut the manila ropes with my Bowie, leaving enough attached to the halters to serve as rein or lead rope.

The black blew.

I froze.

'Hey?' A sleepy voice came from camp.

No time for stealth. I leaped aboard the sorrel and slammed my heels into his ribs. He broke for an opening between two Joshua trees and headed for the plain at a run. The black had no choice but to follow. The third horse, a dark bay, tried to join his mates, but the picket rope stopped him short.

Something clipped a thorn finger from a nearby cholla. A rifle barked. We dipped into a gully and out of sight.

'Sumbitch's stole our horses!' Rifles fired in my general direction, but it was still too dark for accurate shooting. I gave the sorrel its head. The horse could make his way through the desert plant life better than I could guide him.

When we reached Zeeb, I changed mounts. I led the livery horses out into the plains away from Tinajas Altos, away from Ehrenburg, away from any water.

The sun was high overhead when I cut the picket ropes from the halters. The horses would make their way home, or they wouldn't ... or John Walker would find them.

I turned Zeeb's head toward Adam's Well.

3

Long into the night Sean Fowley stared at the constellations in the blue-black sky. When he lay on his side his hip and shoulder joints pained him. When he turned onto his back the pain shifted to his tailbone.

Damn Reed. Damn him to hell. Still, Sean Fowley could not allow a half-Indian 'breed to wound his son and walk away; he had to pay.

Desert dust coated his throat. The insides of his thighs burned. His butt felt bruised from so many hours in the saddle. He longed for a swig of good Irish whiskey, just to clear the phlegm.

A cricket chirped in the brush. A small animal rustled through the chamise. Everything sounded unnaturally loud in the clear desert air, even the methodical chewing of Walker's horse. Fowley shifted again. *Holy*

Mother. Is there not a comfortable spot for a man to lay down in this god-forsaken desert?

Two yards away Bud snorted, then settled into rhythmic snores. Fowley's large son was not a man to take into hostile Indian country.

A shadow knelt at Bud's side. John Walker placed a hand over Bud's nose and mouth. Bud's eyes flew open, but before he could react, Walker spoke. 'It's better not to snore, my friend. Some say the Apaches are at peace, but they can never say for sure. Let's be safe.'

Bud nodded and turned onto his side. The shadow disappeared, leaving only the faint odor of charred grease-wood. Fowley went back to star-gazing.

At some point, Fowley slept.

A horseshoe clicked on stone. One of the Fowleys' mounts blew. Bud scrambled to his feet, rifle in hand. 'Hey!' He fired toward the horses. Pounding hoofbeats followed the rifle shot. Fowley grabbed his own Winchester and jacked a shell into the chamber.

He fired toward the fading sound of running horses.

'Don't waste your cartridges.' John Walker spoke in a quiet voice, but the words cut the darkness like cold steel. 'Now the man you call Breed has your horses.'

Thad ran into camp to face three rifles. 'Wha . . . What's going on? I couldn't hear a thing from up there. Didn't see nothing either.'

'Shit.' Sean Fowley swore. He'd come into the desert on a quick ride to punish a dirty 'breed for hurting his son. Here he was, God only knows how far from Ehrenburg, or any other town, without horses. What good was John Walker anyway? Fowley hired Walker because everybody in town knew he was the best on a trail. If he was the best, how had the 'breed made away with the mounts? All he could think to say was, 'Did the 'breed get all three?'

'Damn that 'breed.' Bud jacked another shell into his new Winchester. The spent brass went spinning to the ground. 'I'm gonna kill that bastard.' He tromped off toward the picket line, sounding more like a troop of infantry than a single man.

Thad watched his father.

Fowley limped back to his blanket, brushed the sand from his socks, and picked up his knee-high boots.

'You'll want to shake those out before putting them on,' Walker said. 'Scorpions like warm, dark places.'

Fowley scowled but shook out one boot and then the other. No scorpion fell out, but a beetle did. It landed on its back, levered itself over, and ambled off toward the chamise at the edge of camp. Fowley stamped his feet into the new boots and winced at how they pinched his toes.

Bud crashed back into camp. 'Da, the bay's still there,' he said. 'Two horses for four men.'

'That is not true,' Walker said. 'I have one horse for myself. You have one horse for three men.' He held his Springfield in the crook of his left arm, his right hand on the action.

Fowley sighed. 'And what do ye say we should do then, boyo?'

'I do not think the 'breed will take the horses far away. You wait here. I will find them. You decide what to do when I return.'

Fowley nodded. 'Do it,' he said.

Walker smiled. 'Think well about trying to punish the 'breed,' he said. He stood for a moment, watching the Fowleys, then strode to his two-color paint. Moments later, he rode out with two canteens, his Springfield, and a converted Navy Colt Model 1861 in a flap holster at his thigh.

Thad busied himself at the grub-sack. He'd naturally taken over as cook when his mother died. He put coffee beans in a cloth bag and beat them into pieces with the butt of his new Remington revolver. The fractured beans went into a six-cup coffee pot full of water from the tanks.

Thad stirred the coals of the cooking fire and added a few sticks of cholla skeleton. Flames soon ate at the dead cactus and heated the coffee pot.

'Coffee in a bit,' Thad said.

'We gotta git that 'breed.' Bud kicked at a fist-sized rock. 'Gotta.'

Sean Fowley agreed with Bud. It would not do to allow a half-breed drifter to get away with overpowering and wounding one of the Fowley family. He'd learned early that a man with power must use it or risk losing it. His father had tenanted on a tiny two-acre piece of Ireland that was owned by an absentee in England and run by a vicious middleman, and paid the rent by working for the owner while raising potatoes on the thin acres to feed his family.

Sean Fowley was a man grown and looking to start a family of his own when the potato blight hit in '45. By the spring of '46, the girl he'd thought to marry was gone to the typhus, and three of his siblings as well.

The middleman, Peadar Dwyer, came around that spring. Jowled and rotund in his tight-fitting tweed coat and flat hat, he could barely get through the narrow front gate. Amos Fowley lay sick abed in the one-room shack when Dwyer arrived. Without removing his hat as a man should, the middleman looked down. 'Yer not paying your rent, Amos Fowley, yer not. So you'll be gone from here by tomorrow, you will.'

Dwyer turned to leave, but stopped at the door. 'Out by tomorrow, ye'll be. I've said it.'

Sean Fowley trembled with impotent rage. He knew better than to hit a middleman, and it was true that Amos Fowley'd been unable to work off the rent over the winter months. A man could do nothing about a middleman.

The Fowleys left their shack and took shelter with a relative in Bellurgan. Eleven people crowded into the little one-room house. A roof they had, but the potatoes still rotted with the blight. Yet there was song and laughter under that roof of an evening.

Uncle Thaddeus returned from market with a huge smile on his face. Amos still lay abed, but Sean did more than a man's share. It was to him that Thaddeus spoke.

'There's a man in town looking for healthy lads to go to America, there is.'

'I have na money, Uncle, I don't. No way to go so far.'

'That's the thing, Sean. He'll pay, or so he said.'

Sean frowned.

'A chance for you, it is,' his uncle said. 'Working in America, you could send a bit of money back to your da and the kiddies, I'd say.'

'Any place would be better than Bellurgan,' Sean said.

Sean Fowley sailed, an indentured man, to New York in a coffin ship. Now he stared into the hatful of fire his son Thad used to brew coffee in the Mojave Desert.

'What'll we do?' Thad asked.

Sean Fowley turned his seamed face to his youngest son. 'No blimey half-breed bastie can lord it over a Fowley,' he growled. 'We will find a way to take him down, that we will.'

'We've got only one horse, Da.'

'I could ride on ahead,' Bud said. 'The breed won't be looking for someone to follow him now.'

'And you think you could do this thing?'

Bud wouldn't meet his father's eyes. 'I can,' he said. 'I must.'

'Then when it's light enough you go if you will. Thaddeus and myself will wait here for Walker. I've said it.'

The Fowleys sat around the tiny fire, sipping at the bitter coffee young Thad brewed.

'I wonder how Reed's doing,' Thad said in a thin voice. His face appeared whiter in the gray pre-dawn light.

'He'll not die,' Fowley said. 'But whether he'll use that right arm again, God only knows.'

'We could go home.'

Fowley growled deep in his chest. 'You'll not say such a thing, Thaddeus.

A Fowley does not give up on something he's set his mind to doing, he don't.'

Thad ducked his head and studied the grounds in the bottom of his coffee cup.

As the sky lightened, the desert began to stir. A cactus wren landed on the willow and surveyed the camp with keen eyes. Somewhere in the rocks above doves chortled. A slight breeze came up, rustling leaves as it blew. Out in the basin, a lone column of smoke climbed skyward.

★　★　★

After turning the livery horses loose, I didn't see any reason to hide my trail. If the Fowleys chose to follow me, they'd be on foot, and townsmen don't make good foot soldiers.

I found a dead mesquite about half a mile from the well, and soon had an armful of sticks chopped for Blessing's fire.

'Thank you, mister,' she said.

A fragrance of chilli rose from the small cast-iron pot she had resting on a tripod of rocks over a pile of coals. She'd chopped the cottontail's remains into chunks and fed them to the bean pot. But no coffee pot sat beside the fire.

'Coffee?' I said.

'Got none.' Blessing sounded apologetic.

Polly watched us askance, as if she didn't want me to notice that she was looking. Garfield didn't move under his hat. I wondered what kind of pimp he was.

'How do you all plan to get where you're going, Blessing?'

She shrugged. 'I cook and wash and clean and stuff. I ride the wagon when it moves.' She dished beans and rabbit into a tin plate and carried it to Garfield. He lifted his hat and took the plate and spoon without a word.

Blessing took another plate to Polly.

'A glass of water, too, bitch.'

'Yes, Miss Polly. Right away.' Blessing found a glass in the wagon, filled it from the water sack, and offered it to Polly. The whore took the glass with a pout.

'I'm not used to eating without a table,' she said.

Blessing handed me a portion. Almighty little was left in the pot. I scraped half of mine back in. 'I can eat off the desert,' I said. 'Just a taste is enough for me.'

Blessing's eyes glistened. She bowed her head, then took the pot to the wagon tailgate, where she shovelled beans and rabbit into her mouth as if she were afraid someone would take the food away from her.

'Don't you eat us all into starvation, now.' Polly's voice was hard and commanding.

'She's only eating my leftovers,' I said,

Polly glared at me. Garfield paid no mind. He was starting to annoy me. A man and two women sat at Adam's Well with a wheel-broke wagon. Far as I could see, Garfield didn't care. He didn't even try to get him and his people out of the fix they were in. What kind of man was he?

By rights I should fork Zeeb and leave. But somehow I couldn't walk out on that skinny little girl. No way to repair that broken wheel, not with just my Bowie and the hand axe, anyway. I strode over to where Garfield sprawled with his back against the willow tree. 'How do you figure to get your women folk outta here, Garfield?' I said.

He tipped his hat back and gave me a hard look. 'Don't see as that's any of your concern, 'breed, 'less you wanna pay for a poke.'

'That wagon wheel ain't gonna fix itself,' I said.

He stared at me a minute, then nodded. He said nothing.

'Food's near gone, ain't it?'

He nodded again.

'Where you headed?'

'Aztec.'

'That's some ways. You'll have to leave the wagon.'

'All we've got's in there,' he said. 'Can't leave it all behind.'

'Can't use nothing if you're dead.'

He just sat there.

'You're the man. You gotta decide.'

His mouth set in a hard line and his brow furrowed. 'I can't,' he said, his voice pitched low. 'I planned to wait here till someone came by with a wagon.'

'People stop by the well, I'll grant you that. But I wouldn't bank on anyone coming with an empty wagon. Not before you all starve anyway.'

Both Polly and Blessing held stock still, hardly breathing, listening hard to what Garfield had to say.

Garfield took a deep breath. He held it for a moment, then let it out slow. 'I reckon we'll stay here,' he said. 'Someone's bound to show up.'

I could see the fear in his eyes.

'Whoever stops here'll be going to Ehrenberg or Wickenburg, or on to

California,' I said. 'Won't be no one headed for Aztec. That place is no more than a wet stop on the Southern Pacific.'

Garfield half-grinned. 'Know that. Them trains take half- to three-quarters of an hour to fill up with water. That's time for a bunch of pokes with Polly if the gents line up. Maybe even Blessing, though I ain't used her yet. We'll see how business goes. I'll need that wagon, you see.'

I couldn't say another word. All I could do was saddle up and leave. Next man through could well find all three dead. But it weren't up to me. I'd had my say and Garfield wasn't buying.

Zeeb and I rode out with two canteens of water and what little coffee I had left. I slanted east northeast across the desert, aiming for Gila Bend, but I didn't know Blessing followed.

4

From the foothills of the Castle Dome Range, the desert floor looked flat, covered with the light tan of cholla, the dusky green of yucca, and clumps of darker growth that meant prickly pear or hedgehog cholla. Here and there showed the dark green of Joshua trees and paloverde and, far off, three big cottonwoods, a sure sign of water.

Cottonball clouds marched north in east-west lines. They showed no grey underbellies that might mean rain, and they were too far apart to give relief from the white-hot sun. A redtail hawk sailed the updrafts but nothing moved in the morning heat.

I lay on the back side of an up-cropping, watching the lie of the land. It always pays to take the time to look careful before moving out.

All morning I kept to the cover of a

nest of rocks on the up-cropping. Earlier I'd caught sight of a line of Jicarillas moving single file along a wash: six men, four women and four children, including an infant in a cradleboard on one woman's back. Not a hunting party, not a war party, but still not something a man wants to call the attention of. They moved north. Jicarilla Apaches made life tough around Vulture City, I'd heard. I sat still long after they were gone.

Why'd you have to leave such a plain trail? I asked myself. I knew better than to think myself alone in the desert. I'd just gotten full of myself for getting away with the Fowleys' horses. Damn.

I'd left Zeeb where he could chomp on chamise while I surveyed our way across the open plain. Thirty miles away and directly east of me stood the Plomas Mountains. South of that range, the Eagle Tail Mountains rose in a jagged blue line. I planned to move right between those ranges, all the way to the big bend in the Gila River, more than a hundred miles away.

Zeeb blew. He'd stopped chomping. I started to turn and the arrow came out of nowhere to slam me to the ground. My Winchester clattered down the rocks. I struggled to my feet, grasping for the handle of my Bowie, but my hands didn't seem to work right. Something smashed me above the ear, filling my head with stars. Everything went black.

At first I felt only the pain, but gradually I got to where I could take stock of the situation. I gritted my teeth and used my left hand to explore. Blood caked the side of my head and neck. It had soaked into my canvas shirt, which was pinned to me by an arrow that entered just to the left my spine, missed the bone, and protruded from my side, just below my left elbow. The tip had snapped off when I fell.

I struggled to my knees. A sharp steel arrowhead attached to three inches of shaft lay in the dust. I picked it up. Hardwood shaft. Apache coloring. Could have been the Jicarillas I'd seen earlier? I couldn't focus. My mind wandered.

Zeeb?

I couldn't hear my horse.

Strange. The Apache had left the money belt around my waist, yet he'd taken the bandolier of rifle ammunition I'd worn across my chest.

I looked for my Winchester. Gone. I looked for my horse. Gone. I reached for my Bowie. Gone. No footwear. No weapons. No horse.

The Wickenburg stage road was a good twenty miles north. The Gila River lay nearly thirty miles south. The nearest possible place to go was Adam's Well, where Garfield and his whore . . . and Blessing . . . camped.

Right now, I could hardly crawl, much less walk on tender feet for the dozen miles that separated me from Garfield and the women. And I wasn't going anywhere with an arrow through my back and my head threatening to burst open if I moved too sudden.

Damn.

I couldn't see any other way. The arrow had to come out. My whole back throbbed. I knelt and backed up against a big rock sideways. Gritting my teeth, I pushed the fletched end of the arrow against the rock and put my weight on it. The shaft moved a little and sweat popped out all over me. I couldn't bite back the groan that built up from inside. Blood started dribbling down my side. I needed to shuck the shirt, but it couldn't come off until I got the arrow out.

Deep breaths told me the arrow hadn't nicked a lung. I clamped my teeth and pushed again.

The arrow slid easier now it was lubricated with blood. When a good three inches stuck out from under my ribs, I hooked the fletched end of the arrow over a rock lip and dropped. My weight, although no more than 140 pounds after a big meal, bore on the shaft, and it snapped. I saw red and I bled, but the fletched end of the arrow lay beside me on the hard ground. I kept still, bleeding, willing the pain to go away. It didn't, but after a time, I was able to stand it.

The canvas shirt had to come off, bloody as it was. I undid the buttons with my left hand and shrugged out of the left sleeve first. My head wanted to split open. I worked at focusing on what I had to do, but my thoughts wandered. A *zopilote* buzzard lit on the tallest rock. It'd be after my flesh if ever I stopped moving. Another flapped to a little rise not twenty feet away. It folded its wings and settled down to wait for what it figured in its bird mind was a sure-thing meal.

I had to move. Still, the arrow shaft had to come out. I struggled with the shirt and finally got it off.

The rock I leaned against was hard, but felt good. Even though I hurt, I wanted to sleep. The buzzard on the mound raised his wings and walked two steps closer. The one on the rock just watched. They hoped I'd die.

Gingerly, I raised my right hand to

the protruding end of the shaft. The move took all my strength. I wanted nothing more than to just let my hand flop to the ground so I could rest my head against the rock and maybe black out. I made a fist, thumb and forefinger against my side, grasping the arrow shaft.

Biting my lip and turning the shaft back and forth with wrist movement, I slowly brought the blood-slick arrow out. It parted from my flesh with a sucking sound. Without the strength to toss it away, I let the shaft drop to the ground.

The exit wound seemed to pucker and close up. The bleeding slowed, then stopped. Bluetailed blowflies gathered, licking at the gore and laying eggs God knows where. I'd be lucky if I didn't get screwworms.

Getting the arrow shaft from my body didn't help my head. God, it would be good to sleep.

I struggled to my feet and the two buzzards took off. They joined the other half-dozen or so that soared in lazy circles above me.

The Apache had brained me with something blunt, probably a club. It had raised a huge lump and split my scalp, which bled a bunch. Lucky the brave was more interested in my rifle and cartridges, moccasins and pony than in making sure I was dead. Perhaps he figured the desert would finish the job.

Bits of rock bit into the soles of my naked feet.

The brave took my Bowie along with the rest of the booty. The only thing I had that resembled a weapon or tool was a three-inch length of shaft with a steel arrowhead attached. I picked it up and tested the edges against my forearm. They were sharp.

Three steps and I had to sit down. Flies buzzed. I reckon I was a banquet to them. After a moment, I raised my head, sucking in a deep breath against the pain. An unnatural shape in a crevice caught my eye. My army field glasses! Maybe things were not as bleak as they seemed.

Shadows out on the desert lengthened. The breath of breeze felt cooler. The desert is not a place to wander through in bare feet, but I had to walk. As soon as the sun set, I'd walk. I promised myself I'd walk. With hands not entirely steady, I lifted the field glasses.

I started close to the bottom of the up-cropping rocks and slowly lifted the glasses so I could see a little further each time. Two things caught my interest — a clump of prickly-pear and a packrat's nest.

My shirt lay on the ground where I'd dropped it. I groaned as I bent to pick it up. Throbs of pain traced every heartbeat, starting in the middle of my back and exploding through the knot above my ear. I managed to hold on to the shirt as I straightened up. After a long moment, I started walking toward the prickly-pear clump.

Each step meant placing a foot on

the ground ahead and feeling for sharp stones or cactus spines before shifting my weight to it. While the clump was no more than a quarter of a mile away, the sun had settled on the horizon by the time I got there.

The arrowhead sliced through prickly pear ears like it was a paring knife, and its sharpened edges made short work of the spine clusters. I split the ear and scraped out a thimbleful of cactus flesh with my fingers, then smeared the pulp over the wounds in my side, back, and head.

The sap soon dried and prevented blowflies from laying eggs in my open wounds. The pulp and sap soothed. I took a deep breath and found I didn't hurt as much.

I looked at the packrat nest, a huge mound of twigs and branches. I needed to go there, but my sore feet didn't feel like moving.

The walk to the rat nest took longer than the trip to the prickly pear. While I was on my way, the sunset faded and the desert darkened.

Leaves and husks and bits of bark fall from the twigs a packrat puts on its nest, forming a soft layer of humus beneath the stack of sticks. I pulled them away, spread my shirt, lay on the soft humus, and covered myself with the dried twigs and branches. They'd help keep me out of sight. Head on my left arm, I slept, no longer worried that buzzards would peck at me in my sleep.

★　★　★

Bud returned before John Walker got back with the horses.

'Tracks ain't that easy to follow,' he said. He'd not been gone half a day.

Sean Fowley said nothing. He didn't even look at his son. *What kind of man have I raised?* he thought.

'Coffee?' Thad held a steaming tin cup out to Bud.

'Goldam desert's got to be a hundert 'n' ten, and you give me hot coffee.' Bud took the mug and sipped at the brew. 'Tastes like mud,' he said.

'Water in the tanks is getting low,' Thad said. 'I let it sit to settle the mud out, but it tastes still the same. Nothing else I can do.'

'Goldam desert. God-forsaken waste, it is. A man can't see his way through and them jumping cactuses got eyes, I swear. Shit. Damn. Breed asshole.'

'Hold your tongue, Bud,' Fowley said. 'You'll not catch that man with blaspheme, that you won't. We will wait for John Walker.'

Bud sat on one of the rocks Thad had pulled over near the fire. He stared into his coffee cup, his face morose. He muttered under his breath.

'We could go back to Ehrenburg, Pa,' Thad said in a thin voice.

Fowley glowered. 'We'll not let a half-breed drifter take liberties with a Fowley,' he said. 'That's final.'

Thad nodded, but his face said he didn't like what his father set out to do.

He'll learn, Fowley thought, *just like*

I learned all those years ago in New York.

Fowley had been new off the boat then, knowing nothing of the big land he'd come to.

'You'll put your things here, you will,' Kevin O'Reilly said. He pointed to a dank corner of the dark cellar beneath O'Reilly's Shamrock Pub. 'Don't ya be wastin' your time, boyo. There be work aplenty to do.'

Fowley worked. He swabbed out the pub after the last tipsy Irishman left. He straightened up and restocked the bar, wheeling in new kegs of beer and barrels of what went for Irish whiskey. He snatched moments of sleep in his dank corner, and bathed once a week in a barrel behind the pub. After six months he'd saved enough to buy a second shirt and pair of trousers.

O'Reilly's Shamrock squatted on Little Water Street, facing Paradise Square. Drinks cost little, and O'Reilly often let customers pay off their bills in kind instead of cash. Where the vases and silverware came from or went, Fowley never knew.

'Yer a big man, Sean Fowley, that y'are,' O'Reilly said. 'You be in America two years now and I like the way you handle your shillelagh. That, and I've yet to see you with too much drink.'

Fowley ducked his head. He'd never been one for drunkenness. He liked to keep control of himself. 'I be not terrible fond of poteen, begging your pardon, sir.'

O'Reilly nodded. 'From today, ye'll watch and protect the Shamrock, young Fowley. You'll be one of Carrig Nolan's boys. Ye'll learn it all from him, you will.' O'Reilly turned to go, then faced Fowley again. 'You'll be earning a dollar a week now,' he said, 'and there's a little job I've got for you right this moment.' O'Reilly's eyes held a twinkle.

'You know I'll do it,' Fowley said. 'Whatever the job.' He stood a little taller, happy to have earned O'Reilly's trust. 'What will it be, then,' he asked.

'Me niece Meaghan Donovan lives at

Mott Street,' O'Reilly said. 'She's been visiting herself and is now ready to go home. It's a fair piece and the Daybreak Boys may be around. I'd take it as a personal favor if you'd see Meaghan home safe, I would.'

'I'll see to it, Kevin O'Reilly,' Fowley said.

'Meaghan,' O'Reilly called.

'Out here, Uncle.' The husky voice came from outside the Shamrock. 'T'wouldn't be seemly for an upright woman such as myself to venture into a saloon.'

O'Reilly spoke to Fowley in an undertone. 'A mind of her own, she's got,' he said.

'I'll watch her,' Fowley said. 'You can be sure of it.'

O'Reilly cuffed Fowley on the shoulder. 'I know that, boyo. Else I wouldna ask, would I? Now go.'

Fowley went out the front door of the Shamrock to where Meaghan Donovan waited. He stopped short when he saw her, struck dumb by her fresh-washed beauty. Her pert nose was sprinkled with freckles, and her wide-spread blue eyes were large enough for a man to lose himself in them. Her clothing properly hid her body, but Fowley could imagine her womanly curves beneath the layers of cotton and linen cloth.

'My but ain't you a strapping man?' Meaghan's grin showed in impish nature.

Fowley put a finger to the bill of his flat cap. 'Pleasure, Miss Meaghan. Your uncle says I'm to see you safe to the tenement on Mott Street.'

Meaghan reached for Fowley's arm, but he pulled away. 'We're not betrothed, Miss. 'T'wouldn't be right allowing my boss's niece to hang onto my arm. Come along, now. We'll get you home, we will.'

'As you say, good sir. Let us be on our way, then.' Meaghan started walking north on Little Water Street.

'Miss.'

Meaghan stopped.

'You will stay a step behind me and

61

to the outside. I'll handle anything that may come from the buildings or the alleys. You keep your eye on the traffic, do you. Let us be off now.'

They walked down Little Water Street, then through the Five Points on Cross Street. The mud, manure, human refuse, and slops along the way made high-topped shoes a necessity. To Fowley and Meaghan, however, the rank smell was the unmistakable odor of the Bowery.

Cross Street abutted Mott Street, which led downhill to the tenement, located in the swampy lowland of the former Collect Pond.

'Hey, Mick!'

Fowley reacted by pulling Meaghan close behind him and reaching for the shillelagh he habitually carried stuffed under his belt at the small of his back. 'Who'll be asking?' he said.

Four burly men stepped into the street ahead of Fowley and Meaghan. 'This is Daybreak Boys territory now, Mick, and we'll be teaching you to stay in your own place.'

Fowley made no answer. He merely watched the four spread out and stalk toward him. He shifted his grip on the shillelagh and pushed Meaghan into a corner formed by one building protruding further toward the street than its neighbor. 'Stay here,' he said.

The shillelagh in Fowley's hand became a living thing. It darted out and connected with the point of the nearest Daybreak Boy's jaw. The crack of splintering bone sounded loud in the instant of silence following the blow. Then the man screamed and fell to his knees, clutching his broken face.

'Now ye'll pay, bastard Mick,' yelled another Boy, charging Fowley with a six-inch knife held low.

Fowley grinned like a death mask. His oaken shillelagh swept through the air with an audible swish to smash into the forearm of the Boy's knife arm. The weapon went spinning and Fowley backhanded his truncheon to the side of the Boy's head. He crumpled like a bundle of rags topped by his silk top hat.

Now the odds were only two to one, and Fowley's face wore a steel-hard mask of hate.

'Ye'll not touch one of mine, bugger boys,' he growled. 'Come on. Taste me shillelagh of good oak. Try to chastise this Mick.' He stared at each Daybreak Boy's face. These men he would not forget.

They hesitated.

'Fight, or be gone,' Fowley roared.

They ran.

★   ★   ★

At the camp near Tinajas Altos, Fowley tasted the victory of that long-ago fight. He remembered rallying a gang of Roach Guards and hunting the offending Daybreak Boys down and destroying them. When someone pushed your boundaries, they must be destroyed. Fowley considered his two sons and laid plans to destroy the man called Breed.

5

Whether I slept or passed out, I do not know, but I struggled back to consciousness in the light of morning. I pried my eyes open a slit to bright sunlight and the bake-oven heat of the desert day. Lost blood took what little moisture my body had, and my tongue felt like a dry stick in the cavern of my mouth.

I closed my eyes again and tried to think past the throbbing in my head and the hot iron running through my back. I had to move, else I'd wither up and decorate the packrat's nest as a bundle of bones.

Sticks clattered in the quiet morning as I fought to sit up. A wren peeped from its perch on a creosote bush. The sun inched higher and hotter.

I sat. Then, after ages, I stood. I even leaned down to pick up my shirt. A wounded man should move. Move and you find ways to keep on moving. Give up, lie down, and you just might never get up again.

The field glasses and the front end of the Apache arrow nestled together as if I'd carefully placed them there before going to sleep, but I didn't remember doing it.

With tentative fingers, I explored my wounds. Although the path the arrow made through my body burned and throbbed, the surface wounds had closed and begun to scab over. The lump over my ear had nearly subsided, and the laceration didn't bleed. I shrugged into my shirt. If I could get food and moisture, my wounds would heal.

Food. I'd lathered my wounds with prickly pear pulp and sap before burrowing into the packrat's nest. Prickly pear meant food, too. I picked up the arrow and the field glasses and made my way back to the cactus on tender feet.

I needed food, but rushing to the source would damage my bare feet. Instead, I placed each foot carefully, avoiding sharp bits of sandstone and wayward cholla thorns.

By the time I reached the prickly-pear clump, the sun had risen to its full strength. I'd need to shade up before long, but at the moment, food was my biggest concern.

A few of the cactus pears showed tinges of red. They'd be tart but edible. I twisted a few off and brushed the hair-like spines off against my britches. After half a dozen, I could eat no more. The moist pears refreshed me, but weren't water enough. I needed a barrel cactus. I needed shade. I needed a pair of shoes. And I needed meat if my body was to heal itself.

The prickly-pear maze spread over a slight rise in the desert floor so I could see across the land for some distance. I lifted the field glasses, which hung by a strap around my neck, divided the desert into sections in my mind, and carefully inspected each. Even then, I almost missed the smoke.

It's hard to tell how far away things are in the desert. Mountains that seem near by in the clear, dry air may be fifty miles away. The smoke looked close, a thin column that rose straight for a hundred feet or so, then horse-tailed off to the south on a breath of wind.

I made up my mind to get to the fire. Even if no one was there, I needed it. I set landmarks to lead the way and set off. Bits of rock chewed at my feet, but I plunged on. The flames seemed to burn within me. The most important thing in my life was to reach the fire, even if only ashes remained when I got there.

The soles of my feet didn't last long. Soon I left bloody footprints on the desert earth. My back never let me forget an arrow had pierced it, and the whole side of my head throbbed. The sun burned hot and blinding. My lower lip cracked. I had no saliva to wet it. Mouth open, I sucked hot dry air into my lungs, and more of my body's moisture escaped with each exhaling breath.

Still, I plowed forward, my eyes on the tendril of smoke that rose into the still air. I had to reach the fire. I had to.

Folks say Yuma is so close to Hell that a man can dig down two feet and hear voices. The fires of Hell would have been a relief from the heat of the wicked sun over the Mojave Desert. Blood loss and only half a dozen prickly pear fruit in my belly didn't give me much strength.

The first time I fell to my knees the smoke was yet a long way off. I stayed for a moment, panting at the dry air and gathering what little gumph I had. I lunged to my feet and staggered a step or two. My whole body was a pool of pain, so the prickles in my feet added little. I ignored them. The tendril of smoke still rose, much closer than it had been when I decided to find its source.

I checked the landmarks I'd set when

starting out. I'd passed two of them. A giant saguaro stood off to my left, the third landmark of the four. I hobbled onward, and after an eternity, the big cactus fell behind.

The smoke still rose, much closer now.

I felt broiled. Skewered and broiled. My dark Cheyenne heritage kept me from burning like a white man, but without a hat the tops of my ears roasted first, along with the bridge of my nose. Long sleeves and denim Levis protected my body. The arches of my feet would soon blister.

A sandstone spire, my fourth landmark, showed on my right. I squinted, trying to see through the shimmering heat waves. Far off, a lake spread along the foothills of the Plomas Mountains. I knew it for a mirage. It still made me long for water.

I stumbled on, the spire to my right, and nearly stepped off into a deep arroyo. It twisted south, and beyond the bend the smoke rose skyward.

The field glasses hung from my neck like a lump of lead. I wanted to drop the weight but deep in the fog of my mind, something made me keep them.

From where I stood, the sides of the gorge dropped away in steep sandstone cliffs at least fifty feet high. I could only follow the banks of the arroyo as it wound south. Forcing my battered feet to walk, I limped ahead, my eye on the wavering smoke. My Cheyenne blood warned me to take cover. My body could barely move, much less slink. I staggered on.

I counted my paces to keep myself focused on the trail. At one hundred and eight steps, part of the sandstone side of the arroyo had given way and a slide of rock and sand fanned out into the little canyon. A way down. Steep and probably dangerous, but a way down. I squinted. A hint of smoke still drifted upwards.

With arrow in hand and the field glasses secure around my neck, I sat on the bank of the arroyo and inched myself toward the sand slide. The first few feet went over solid rock, then the beginnings of the rubble. Once I got onto that runway of sand and rock, I couldn't have stopped if I'd wanted, and without shoes, my feet made useless brakes. The angle toward the bottom steepened and I plummeted downward. All I could do was try to keep in the middle of the rubble. I lost control. Tumbled. Rolled.

Near the bottom, I sailed off a ten-foot section of remaining cliff, flailed through the air, to land on my right side. The sand broke the fall but the impact still knocked the wind out of me. The sun declined west as I sought the smoke and now the bottom of the arroyo was half in shadow. I lay for a time in the sweet shade of the arroyo bank, then rolled over and rose to my knees.

My head hung. It felt like someone was inside, banging on my skull with a twelve-pound sledge. Someone else ran a white-hot poker through my back.

The smoke. Had to get to the smoke. Somehow I got to my feet.

Walk is not the right word for what I did. Still, I made progress. No sign of smoke now, but I knew it had to be just around the next twist in the arroyo. It had to be there.

Head down, eyes on the ground, I wobbled down the arroyo, scarcely aware of anything but the need to find the smoke.

The arroyo sank deeper into the shadow as the sun slid west. I panted through dry and cracking lips. The smoke. If only I could find the smoke, everything would be OK.

I stumbled and sprawled on the rocky trail. Trail? Without noticing, I'd started following a trail.

My palms bled from breaking my fall, but the drops were dark and thick. I couldn't get up, so I crawled. I picked a white-faced rock ahead and crawled to it. Beyond the rock, a red piece of sandstone. I inched my way to it. I saw a patch of black on the arroyo floor. It became my goal. I only had to get that far.

Move an inch. Another. The black spot got closer. Eventually, I got to where I could reach out and touch it — the remains of a fire that had been set so sticks would fall into it as the flames burned down. It was dead, the smoke gone. Nothing. No one. Only the lifeless remains I'd spent so much to find.

The fight to survive leaked from me. I lay down by the dead fire and closed my eyes. I had no idea if I'd ever open them again.

      ★   ★   ★

'Mister?'

I heard the voice from a long way off.

'Mister?'

Blessing? Couldn't be. She was stuck at Adam's Well with that no-good pimp.

'Mister? Can you hear me? Mister?'

I cracked an eyelid. The light flickered and the shadows danced. *Who are you?* I meant to say, but could only croak. A face swam into focus. Blessing. I wanted to say, *My God. What are you doing here?* I made two croaks instead of one. Blessing smiled. She poured a little water over my lips and some of it leaked into my mouth. Lukewarm. A trickle. Marvellously wet. I couldn't swallow so I just let the water slip into the back of my throat where the dry tissues soaked it up. I croaked again, and Blessing gave me more water. I swallowed.

'Blessing?' I said, tearing at the dryness in my throat.

'Don't talk, mister.' She poured more water. I swallowed again. Then I noticed Blessing was not alone.

I struggled to sit up and found that I was lying with my head in Blessing's lap, surrounded by what looked to me like half the Apache nation.

'*Dáazho,*' I mumbled.

'*Dáazho,*' the Apaches chorused.

'Mister?'

My voice finally worked. 'Blessing?

What in hell are you doing here?'

She looked mortified that I'd ask. 'Some men came to Adam's Well,' she said. 'They took Garfield's horses and our food and left. Mr Garfield and Miss Polly wouldn't leave the well, so I came alone.'

'Came?'

She nodded. 'I walked and walked and when I got far enough away from Adam's Well, I lit a fire and made smoke.'

'I followed your smoke, then?'

Blessing nodded. 'But the smoke was not for you.'

I glanced at the ring of silent warriors. 'Them?'

She ducked her head like she was embarrassed. 'Yes,' she said.

'Why?'

'When I was a little girl — I don't remember all that much — but when I was a little girl, my family travelled with a wagon train that was following the Mormon Battalion Trail from Santa Fe to California. About then,

76

some Mexicans massacred a Mescalero Apache rancheria in the Chiricahua Mountains and the tribe wanted revenge. Some young warriors attacked our wagon train and killed everyone except five children. I was the youngest. Chief Puma saw me at the Mescalero camp and traded two fine ponies for me. He called me Lolotea. I have no idea what my real whiteman's name is. The closest translation of the name Chief Puma gave me is Blessing.

She searched my face. I held it without expression. She resumed her story.

'When I was about twelve, Chief Puma decided I would be better off living with white men. He took me to Fort Huachuca and told them he'd traded for me, that he wanted to give me back to my people.'

'And you ended up with Garfield?'

Blessing nodded. 'No one wants a girl that grew up with Indians,' she said.

I tried to smile. 'Something like being

a half-breed, maybe.'

A little water makes a big difference. After half a dozen swallows, some of the pain let up. The guy in my head with the sledge-hammer went away. My back stayed stiff and sore, but the hot poker pulled out. My bruised and bloody feet became the biggest hurt, but they'd heal. Water just might be the best medicine of all, especially from the hand of a woman as good-looking as Blessing. I wondered if she had a family name. But then, I'd not told her mine.

I sat up and crossed my legs. A small fire burned where the smoke had risen. Four Jicarilla Apaches sat across the fire from me. When they saw I'd joined humanity, one stood and disappeared into the darkness.

'What do the Apaches want?' I said to Blessing in an undertone.

'They're family,' she said.

'Family?'

'Chief Puma and his three sons. My Apache father and brothers.'

The one who left came back and sat

down. The sons looked young, in their teens, perhaps. I'd only glanced at them, but now I took a good look. Then another. The middle son, the one who'd gone and returned, cradled a rifle in the crook of his left arm and it looked an awful lot like my one-in-a-thousand Winchester '73.

'That boy's got my rifle,' I muttered to Blessing.

She looked at me, then nodded.

'Your family shot me, took my rifle and Bowie, my moccasins and my hat, and left me to die in the desert,' I said. 'Your brothers can't claim to be friendly, any way you look at it.'

The old man spoke. 'Yudisthir.' He used my Apache name. 'My son Gosheven counted coup on you. He took your rifle and your horse as rightful plunder.' The chief held out a pair of cactus moccasins. Mine. 'If you wish to recover your other belongings, you must contend with Gosheven in the Circle of the Knife.'

I knew of the Apache custom of tying

warriors together and letting them fight for supremacy. Death was part of life, and the Circle of the Knife was usually fought until one of the contestants died.

Chief Puma continued. 'Yudasthir, what is your decision?'

The youngster's eyes glittered. He wanted to fight. If he won, bragging rights would be his for weeks, maybe months. His reputation as a warrior would leap ahead. He was a boy, but he'd been raised an Apache. The fight would be no pushover. 'I will enter the Circle of the Knife,' I said, and wished my back didn't hurt so much.

6

Except for John Walker, the Fowleys rode into La Paz looking more like scarecrows than a posse out to chastise a wayward half-breed. Fowley's grim face wore a mask of desert dust. Cracks showed along the lines of his brow and the slashes that ran from his nostrils to the corners of his downturned mouth. Nearly two weeks of stubble and dust turned his cheeks gray-black. From deep beneath his brows Fowley's eyes burned like blue fire. Reins clasped in his right fist, he guided the livery bay to the stable.

Bud and Thad rode Garfield's tired team bareback. They'd long ago abandoned the shiny new shotgun chaps and forked the horses gingerly on raw butts and thighs.

At the stable, Fowley turned his fiery eyes toward John Walker. 'Take the team back to Adam's Well, John, if you would, and do whatever it takes to fix their wagon wheel. I'll not be known as a thief. Come to me when you get back and we'll settle your payment.' He ignored his sons.

Fowley stalked down the street toward the Shamrock, one of the three saloons he owned in La Paz, named after Kevin O'Reilly's pub in New York. 'I'll have a dark beer,' he said to the bartender as he came through the double doors. 'Bring it to my office.'

'Aye, sor,' the barkeep said.

A basin and a pitcher of water stood just outside the back door of the Shamrock. Fowley rolled up his sleeves and sloshed water over his face and arms to rid himself of the Mojave Desert dust he'd eaten for too long. He dried with a scrap of flour sacking and scraped a hand across the stubble on his face. He'd get a shave at Robinson's later. Right now, a bold dark beer waited in his office. His mind went to the 'breed. The bastard had led them into the ground out in the desert. Fowley thought he should have known better. He'd learned from General Meagher during the war that a man should meet the enemy on his own terms.

In the office, seated once again behind his massive oak desk, Fowley quaffed the mug of beer in long hungry swallows. Then he placed the empty mug on the desk and he leaned back in his chair, his hands laced behind his head. He closed his eyes and appeared to doze, but behind the shuttered eyelids his thoughts raced.

Sitting up, Fowley roared. 'Kincaid!'

The side door opened and a slim young man with a green eyeshade entered. 'You called, Mr Fowley?'

'How's Reed?'

'Dr Dysterheft stitched up the arm, sir. The doctor says he'll regain use of it with time.'

Fowley nodded. The news didn't change his mind about the 'breed. The man had to be taken down. The Fowley reputation demanded it.

'I want you to find Dutch Regan,' Fowley said. 'Last I heard, he was in Tombstone. Get hold of Johnny Behan, he'll know.'

'Yes, sir. Have you any message for Mr Regan?'

'I need him here, I do, and quick like. Get on it.'

Kincaid quietly closed the door as he left.

Fowley put the 'breed from his mind. He could do nothing until Dutch Regan arrived.

★   ★   ★

Wounds mean nothing to an Apache. A man is expected to fight on through pain and injury. That's the warrior's way. The Sun Dance of my Cheyenne mother's people is the same. Ignore pain. Dance all day with thongs through your breast muscles. Stare at the sun. Seek the sacred trance. I'd taken an arrow through the back and a

84

stiff blow to the head. Now I had to face Chief Puma's son Gosheven in the Circle of the Knife.

A shadow fell across the sand before me.

'Yudasthir.'

I raised my eyes to meet Puma's.

He held out a hunk of seared meat skewered on a knife. 'You must have food,' he said. 'Eat.'

My eyes focused on the meat. It dripped red, the heat of the tiny smokeless fire the Apaches kindled had done little toward cooking it. I took the hunk, nodding my thanks, and tore at the bloody meat with bared teeth. No salt. Half raw. I'd not tasted more delicious food in the Barbary Coast restaurants of San Francisco. Puma smiled, left, and came back with another barely singed chunk. I devoured that, too. Then I wondered if I was eating Zeeb. Apaches would eat a good horse rather than ride it.

Blessing came with some corny cake, only it was mesquite beans, ground, mixed with water, and baked on a rock. I ate three. Strength flowed into my limbs. I felt like a man again.

'Mister?' Blessing held out a skin container. 'Two swallows, mister,' she said.

I took the skin and up-ended it. Two swallows of *tiswin*, the Apache answer to mescal.

'My father says we must go to his rancheria,' she said. 'Safer there.'

'When do I fight the boy?'

'Later.'

We walked, Puma's eldest son in the lead. I limped, but my cactus moccasins protected my feet and I was soon moving as nimbly as the others.

Late in the afternoon, we stopped in the shade of a stand of cottonwoods. A dry streambed wound around and between the big trees. Gosheven sharpened an iron-wood branch with my Bowie, then dug into the streambed near a small overhang. After a few jabs with the stick he cleared away the sand he'd loosened, and the ground showed damp. Half an hour later he'd dug a hole nearly three feet deep. Water collected in the bottom. We drank all we could hold.

The Apaches lit a fire beneath a huge cottonwood, trusting the foliage to disperse any smoke, I supposed. When it was down to a bed of coals, the boys threw two foot-long lizards on the coals and spitted a cottontail rabbit's carcass on a stick to roast. Blessing spotted a hedgehog cactus and set about making its arms edible. She'd slice off the end of an arm, stick her finger in the core, and cut the spines off like she was trimming the skin off a cucumber. She ended up with about six inches of skinned cactus, which she chopped off and brought to us, one at a time. I ate mine as if it were a cob of corn, chomping the cactus flesh from the stringy core. The flesh was not as crisp as cucumber, and tasted musty, like cactus smells, but it was wet and chewed up well. It made a good addition to charred cottontail meat and strings of flesh plucked from the lizards after the burnt skin had been removed. All in all, ample food and plenty of water. The desert was kind to us.

Puma led us north, across the Ehrenberg-Wickenburg stage road and around the end of the Plomas range. Then we turned east over Granite Wash and headed for the Harcuvar Mountains. We didn't stop at a single known water source, but we never dried out. The eldest son carried a water skin; I never saw anyone drink from it.

Puma toted an old trap-door Springfield. The oldest son had a Yellow Boy Winchester that looked to be .45 caliber. The second son proudly carried my one-in-a-thousand Winchester '73, and the youngest boy had a short bow and half a dozen arrows. He hunted for all of us. I wondered if Gosheven had ditched his bow and arrows when he latched onto my rifle.

Most of the time, Puma, Blessing, and I walked together. The youngsters ranged far out of sight, watching for any sign of danger, I imagined, and bringing back meat for the camp. Blessing harvested the desert, always giving us something fresh and tasty to offset the monotonous fare of broiled game.

We reached Puma's rancheria in the Harcuvar Mountains the afternoon of our third day on the trail. Puma had chosen a small mountain meadow enclosed by granite walls and butting into a blind canyon. No stream ran through the meadow, but grama, lovegrass, and fescue grasses said moisture lay not far beneath. I counted twenty-three wickiups.

I'd spotted three lookouts on the way in. There were probably more.

Blessing borrowed a machete from one of the women and left. Puma motioned for me to follow him. His people parted to let us through. I'd heard that Apaches tend to beat their prisoners. No one touched me. Maybe I wasn't a prisoner.

Three days on the trail did a lot for

my wounds. My head ached hardly at all, but the track the arrow had made through my back was still a path of fire when hit just right. My feet worked well, protected by cactus moccasins.

I was more than happy that Puma had brought us to the Harcuvars. The time did me well. I wasn't fully recovered but Gosheven wasn't full grown. I figured I had more experience than he. That said, Apache boys do nothing that won't be of use when they take the warrior trail. The boy would be no pushover.

'Come,' Puma said, and ducked into a wickiup.

I followed.

'Sit,' he said, motioning toward a place on the swept, hard earthen floor.

I sat cross-legged, facing the fire pit in the center of the wickiup.

Puma lowered himself opposite me with a little groan. 'One hates to grow old,' he said. 'Joints and muscles no longer do as commanded.' His smile looked more like a grimace.

I said nothing.

'Yudasthir.'

'I hear you, my chief,' I said.

'He is young and sometimes fool-hardy,' Puma said.

'Youth are like that. It's what makes a man.'

Puma nodded. 'It does.' He looked at me for some minutes as if trying to see what lay beneath my skin.

'Apaches know of Yudasthir, the man always firm in battle. I wonder if my son can best you in the circle of the knife?'

'I carry the wounds he gave me.'

'Wounds give a warrior will to prevail,' Puma said. 'I must put myself in your debt and risk the scorn of my son forever. I would that he not die at your hand.'

'I may not be able to best him,' I said. 'And losing may hurt him more than death . . . in his own mind, at least.'

Puma showed a tiny smile. 'Yudasthir learned well. It is good that you do not think he is only a boy. At seventeen he has yet to be successful in his vision quest. He has nothing to guide him.'

'Life is difficult,' I said.

'My son is angry. Because he exceeds others in warrior games, he thinks he is better. He cannot see it is the anger that prevents his vision.'

'I'm sorry,' I said. 'He is grown. I will face him as a warrior. *Usen* must decide who prevails.'

Puma nodded. 'What you say is true, Yudasthir,' he said.

A woman called from outside the wickiup. 'Food.'

'We eat,' Puma said. 'Come.'

The woman, Blessing, and Puma's three sons sat around the fire. Puma took his place with his back to the mountains. He motioned for me to sit at his left. The boy Gosheven glared. Sitting at the chief's left hand made me an honored guest.

The meal — porcupine, sego lily bulbs, and wild onions — proceeded in silence. Blessing kept sending me glances from beneath her brows. I didn't know why.

The porcupine tasted faintly of spruce. Not unpleasant, but not for the white man's table. The bulbs and onions were starchy and bland on the tongue. No salt. No pepper. No seasonings of any kind. Perhaps food was better that way.

'Yudasthir is here because of Lolotea's smoke,' Puma said. 'He came though Gosheven's arrow pierced his body and his head bore the mark of Gosheven's club.'

Gosheven glowered.

'Lolotea prepared a *gowa* wickiup.' Puma turned to me. 'You will use the wickiup this night, Yudasthir. When the sun rises, you will face Gosheven in the Circle of the Knife. I have spoken.' Puma stood and looked at each person around the fire. Gosheven would not meet the chief's gaze. He stared at the remains of the fire instead, his face hard and expressionless.

'*Usen* will judge,' Puma said. He left

the fire and entered the wickiup in which we had talked. The woman followed.

Blessing tugged at my sleeve. I went with her to the new wickiup. 'You continue to surprise me, Blessing,' I said.

She smiled. 'It's nothing like a house in Ehrenburg or Prescott,' she said, 'but it's easy to put up and all I have to do when we move is burn it.'

'Simple,' I said. 'My mother's people carry a big hide tipi when they move.'

Blessing nodded. 'Apaches don't need much to have a good life. But for men, fighting is part of living.'

'That's how it is with many men, white or red or black,' I said. 'Half-breeds like me learn to fight early on. Takes that to survive.'

Blessing nodded. 'Women must fight, too,' she said, then changed the subject. 'I borrowed furs from my mother.'

'Puma's wife?'

'Of course. I don't have any of my own and you are my guest.'

I barked a short laugh. 'Your smoke kept me going so you probably saved my life. Tomorrow young Gosheven may take it away.'

'Are you afraid?'

I thought for a moment. I wasn't afraid of Gosheven. Concerned, yes. My body might let me down, but each man must die at his appointed time. *Usen*, the Apache Great Spirit, might tip the sales in Gosheven's favor. 'No,' I said.

Blessing touched me. I'm not a big man, but her hand on my arm looked almighty small. 'Mister,' she said. 'I've got no name but Lolotea, Blessing, which Puma gave me.' She looked up into my face. 'Would it be too much if I asked you to tell me your name?'

I had to laugh. 'I've had so many names,' I said. 'Where do I begin?'

'At the beginning?' Blessing had shed her thin cotton dress for buckskin. She no longer looked frail. The leather gave her strength and the planes of her face held a kind of power.

'I was born in Colorado,' I said, 'at Black Kettle's camp on Sand Creek. My father worked at Bent's Fort until Old Man Bent blew it up in '49. George Bent married the oldest of Black Kettle's daughters: my father married the youngest.'

'So you're Cheyenne, then. My father says the Cheyenne are great horsemen.'

'True.'

I continued. 'From the name my father gave me, the Cheyenne called me *Honiahaka*, the Little Wolf.'

'*Honiahaka*.' She rolled the name on her tongue.

'After Bent destroyed the fort, my father often left to trade in Santa Fe, hunt gold at Pike's Peak, or whatever suited his fancy at the time. We lived with Black Kettle at Sand Creek. I was Cheyenne.'

I squatted at the entrance of Blessing's wickiup and scratched marks in the dirt with a stick. Again I heard the roar of Chivington's guns. Again I saw old Black Kettle standing with his American flag in one hand and a white flag of surrender in the other. That was the day my mother died.

7

Blessing touched my sleeve. 'I'm sorry you lost your mother in such a way,' she said. Tears trickled down her face.

'Chivington was crazy,' I said. 'So was Custer. People come up against something or someone different, they try to change them; turn the different ones into something that looks like themselves. Either that, or kill them all.'

'But they didn't kill you.'

'Still haven't figured out whether that was good luck,' I said, 'or bad.'

She raised her eyebrows.

'I don't look much like a Cheyenne. Chivington's men took me for a captured white kid. They hauled me off to Denver and set about remaking me into a white man. I fought. I ran away. I rightly earned the name they used for me — Wilder. And I was a lot wilder than most.'

'That's your name, then? Wilder?'

'For a while. I still use it of a time,' I said, dabbling in the dirt with the same stick.

'You didn't go back to the Cheyenne?'

'The do-gooders in Denver thought God would favor them if they made a white man out of me. I was a prisoner.' *And I hated it*, I thought.

'Your father? Didn't he return?' Blessing asked her questions in a soft voice that reverberated in my ears.

'They said no one survived Sand Creek. He probably heard. He never showed again. I don't even know his name, though I've not tried to find him either.'

'How sad.'

'Yes, sad.' I removed the money belt and held it out to Blessing. 'One thousand dollars in gold coins,' I said. 'Keep it safe. If I die tomorrow, it's yours. If not, we'll talk about what to do with it.'

She hesitated, searched my face with

darting eyes, then took the belt. 'I will guard it well,' she said, hefting its weight.

'Thank you.'

'I still don't know a name to use when I think of you, when I speak to you in my dreams, when I call out to you in my mind.'

'A tough old sergeant at Fort Weld changed my life and gave me a name. I still use it.'

I stopped talking and my mind wandered over the years to see Sergeant-Major Darragh Regan and his wife Fiona. They already had two sons, grown and gone before I arrived, but they still took me in. The sarn't major made no child of me. He taught me army discipline and got me my first job as a scout with Al Sieber.

'Sergeant-Major Regan gave me the name of Falan. It means wolf in his native tongue. On the white man's records, I'm known as Falan Wilder. My friends call me Fal, or Wolf.'

'And what shall I call you, mister?'

Blessings eyes were large and round, pupils dilated in the darkness.

'Whatever you wish.'

'Then you shall be Wilder to me.' She closed her eyes and sat for a moment in silence. Then she smiled, opened her eyes, and looked up into my face again. 'Wilder,' she said. 'Hmmm. Yes. Wilder.' And she kissed me on the cheek.

★ ★ ★

When the river channel changed and left La Paz high and dry, Ehrenburg became the major loading point for steamers up the Colorado from Yuma and points south. Men and goods flowed through the town like the river itself, and a good share of any cash the men carried ended up in the coffers of a Fowley saloon. Fowley's wife Meaghan succumbed to consumption in '75, despite the family's move to dry Arizona. Her departure left Fowley with three sons to rear. Now each was responsible for a saloon; Fowley made the final decisions and kept a tight grip on the purse strings. Never again would he or any of his face poverty and starvation.

Fowley ate his noontime meal — breakfast for men whose business was most active in the wee hours — in his office with his sons. The meal let Fowley ask questions and allowed Bud, Thad, and Reed to think aloud. Progress often came from Fowley's office at noon.

'Pa, the hoors're wearing out,' Thad said. 'If they get too tired and sloppy, income will suffer.'

'And what would ye have me do, Thaddeus?'

'I hear there's a glut on the Barbary Coast. A thousand dollars in the right hands could get us a couple dozen hoors. I could send the money to Dirk Kavanagh in Frisco. He's got men enough to do the job.'

'Reasonable, that is. Do it.'

Thad nodded, his face flushed with pleasure.

Fowley turned to Bud. 'A fight at the Lucky Seven, I hear?'

'Nothing I can't handle.' As usual, Bud's answer contained a hint of belligerence.

'So what were the damages and who will pay? I want to know.'

'Sheriff Traven's got three men in jail for disturbing the peace. I reckon Judge Whitfall'll make 'em pay.'

'For what?'

'Two smashed chairs and a broken table leg.'

Fowley nodded slowly. 'All right. Be mindful, son, that no saloon profits from a fight. Ye'll want to nip problems before tempers get out of control, you will.'

'I know that, Pa. I wasn't born yesterday.'

'Some days I wonder.'

Reed Fowley sat silent while his brothers reported. He no longer wore his arm in a sling, but a fever burned inside him. No one had found the 'breed who'd cut him, and his lust for revenge ate at his guts.

Fowley turned his attention to his youngest son. 'What was your take, Reed?'

Reed's eyes focused and he seemed to rejoin the group. 'Take? Oh. Not so good, Pa, but not all that bad, either. Fifteen hundred bucks and change in drinks. A couple of hundred clear on the whores. Where's the 'breed?'

Fowley gave Reed a sharp glance. 'Run your saloon, boyo. I'll see to the 'breed.'

'I'm the one he cut. I still can't handle a short gun with my right hand, and I don't shoot lefty worth a damn.'

'You'll know when I find him, and find him I will.' Fowley stared at Reed. 'Don't you believe me, boyo?'

Reed's reply grated between clenched teeth. 'I believe you, Pa, I do.'

'Good.'

A knock came on the door, and it opened to show Kincaid on the threshold. 'Ordinarily I would not bother you during your noon meal, Mr

Fowley, but a man who calls himself Dutch Regan is asking for you. What would you have me do?'

'Dutch?' Fowley's face lit up. 'Give him whatever he wants to drink. Show him in when the clock in the vestibule strikes one.'

The man who strode into Fowley's office dominated the room. He stood only about five-ten, but his shoulders measured an axe handle and a quarter across and his biceps stretched the broadcloth of his frock coat tight across his arms. His square face, bronzed by sun and wind, was clean shaven except for a big walrus moustache. His lips turned up at the corners as if he were perpetually amused. His eyes were bits of blue ice under heavy black brows.

Fowley stood as Regan came in. 'Welcome, Dutch,' he said, 'and I'm thanking you for coming.'

Dutch nodded and sat without invitation. 'You sent an urgent message, Mr Fowley. I'd like to know what you want.'

'Are you still a Pinkerton?'

'No.'

Kincaid knocked and entered. 'The coffee you ordered, Mr Fowley. For two.'

'On the desk.'

Kincaid put the china cups and saucers in place along with a pot of coffee, and left without another word.

Fowley poured the coffee. 'Black?'

'Yes,' Dutch said. 'What do you want? It's only because of my da that I came, you know.'

'He's still with the Army, is he not?'

'Presidio in San Francisco.'

'And your mother?' Fowley tried to make conversation.

Dutch ignored the question. He gulped at the coffee and returned the cup to its saucer with a clank. 'What do you want?'

Fowley cleared his throat. 'Um, I want you to find a man and bring him to me.'

'Name?'

'They seem to call him Breed, they do.'

Dutch's eyes sharpened. 'Breed?'

'The bugger cut my son. I can't let that pass. He must pay.' Fowley's voice sounded flat and hard.

Dutch's lips twitched in a smile that didn't reach his eyes. 'You want me to find a man with no name?'

Fowley said nothing.

'I'd not heard you were a joker,' Dutch said, 'but surely you jest, as they say.'

'I have eyewitnesses. My son Reed can tell you. The bartender, too. And John Walker, when he returns.'

'John Walker? The guy who lives with the Pimas?'

'He's the one. He seemed to know the man called Breed.' Fowley looked hopeful.

'But Walker's not in La Paz.'

'Not at the moment. But he'll be back any time, he will.'

Dutch took a deep breath. 'You're asking a lot, Fowley.' Somewhere, Dutch had dropped the 'Mr'.

'I'll pay.'

Dutch picked up the cup and drained the coffee. The white china looked frail in his thick hand. He sat in silence.

'A thousand dollars,' Fowley said.

Dutch replaced the cup, then folded his arms.

'Two thousand.'

'I'll take the thousand now,' Dutch said. 'You can give me the two thousand when I bring this man called Breed in.'

Fowley swallowed hard, the sound loud in the quiet room. A trickle of laughter came through the door to the saloon. He stood, his face uncertain.

Dutch held Fowley's gaze. 'Chances are there ain't no one else who can find your 'breed, Fowley. You want him, you pay. Else forget about ever seeing him again. Were I him, I'd never come to this town again. You're setting yourself up like a bitty king here, and us Irish lose no love on kings. I'll do this job for you, though, because of my pa.'

Fowley strode to a painting on the wall, pushed it aside, and worked the combination of the wall safe behind the picture. 'Coin or bills,' he asked.

Dutch's smile widened. 'Coin,' he said. 'Always did like gold.'

Fowley scowled at the safe. He didn't like parting with his money, but payback to the 'breed was more important. He sighed silently and lifted the lid of the box that held gold coins — stacks of eagles to the left, double eagles to the right. He counted out the coins and put them in a small canvas pouch. 'Fifty double eagles,' he said, hefting the little sack. 'At five-eighths of an ounce each, you've got two pounds of gold and a little change. You'll want to be careful.'

Dutch snorted. 'In your town? I'd figure everyone from mayor to river-front pimp would know not to bother me.' He paused. 'But if anything does happen to me, Fowley, I'll consider it your fault, and our next meeting might not be as friendly as this one.'

He pocketed the pouch. 'I'll be at the Monarch,' he said. 'You don't own that hotel. Send someone over when you've lined up your witnesses.'

It irritated Fowley that anyone would use such a tone to him, but he needed Dutch Regan, so he let it slide. He would not forget. 'I'll send someone,' he said.

Dutch Regan stalked out of Fowley's office, clomped through the Shamrock as drinkers hastened to get out of his way. He opened the front door, stepped out, and closed it a bit harder than was necessary.

Fowley cursed under his breath. 'Kincaid!' he roared. The assistant's head popped in the side door. 'Here, Mr Fowley.'

'Have that bartender from the Black Diamond here at sundown. See that Reed comes with him. When they get here, call Dutch Regan from the Monarch. He wants to hear what they have to say.'

'Yes, sir.'

Fowley felt better after assigning Kincaid to get things moving. The assistant seemed foppish at first glance, but he always did exactly what Fowley told him to.

★ ★ ★

'You can go,' Dutch said to Reed and Flynn the bartender.

Reed looked at his father, who nodded.

When the two men had shut the door behind them, Dutch stood and started pacing. 'Them two didn't give me a helluva lot to go on, Fowley. A man who called himself Breed. Average height. Slight build. No short gun. Big Bowie. Dark face. Didn't get a good idea why your son decided to toss him. Maybe he don't like people he don't know. Maybe he's just mean. But it don't seem like no way to build a business.'

'Wait for John Walker,' Fowley said.

'OK. You're paying.'

'I am. And I want that man.'

Dutch's smile looked condescending.

'You may not like what you find, Fowley,' he said.

'Enjoy your stay at the Monarch,' Fowley said, 'and try not to spend all those gold coins before Walker gets back.'

'You're a hard man to like, Fowley. Can't really see how my pa managed. But let me tell you this. You come on hard to me and you'll look for someone else to find your breed. That, and whoever you pick won't be half as good as me.'

Fowley gave Dutch a blank stare. 'Why do you think I sent for you, Dutch? I'm used to the best. That's what you are, and that's why I'm paying you three times the going rate, I am. I was not born day before yesterday, now, was I?'

'Kingpins fall, Fowley. You'd best keep that in mind. I'll be at the Monarch, or close by.' Dutch left.

John Walker returned the next day, and he met with Dutch Regan just after noon.

'I'm after what you know about the breed who cut Fowley's boy Reed,' Dutch said.

'I would be pleased to meet you, too, Dutch Regan,' Walker said, 'but I see we are not to be civil in our meeting.'

Dutch scowled, then put on a blander face. 'I know of you, John Walker. All say you are a man of your word and as good in the desert as Yuma or a Mojave. I'm pleased to make your acquaintance.'

Walker looked half-pleased. 'My thanks to you, Dutch Regan. We shall speak as equals, as you are first among manhunters.'

The corners of Dutch's mouth lifted in what could have been a smile. 'Then, John Walker, chief of scouts, what can I learn from you about the 'breed?' He hitched his chair around to face John Walker, who did the same. Dutch pulled an Old Glory cheroot from the inside pocket of his frock coat and lit it with a lucifer scratched into flame on the leg of his chair. He puffed at the slim Old Glory until it had half an inch of ash, then offered it to John Walker. 'Share my smoke,' he said.

'An honor, manhunter,' Walker said. He accepted the cheroot and puffed at it with solemn dignity.

They smoked in silence, ignoring Fowley, who sat glowering behind his desk.

'Your smoke is good, manhunter,' Walker said at last. 'The man called Breed is no fool. He does not kill just because he can. He did not kill Reed Fowley, although he was threatened with a pistol. He did not kill Bud Fowley, although he could have shot the man instead of the canteen.'

Dutch smoked at his cheroot, saying nothing. He kept his eyes on Walker's face.

'The 'breed recognized who was trailing him, so he doubled back to talk to me, and then to Fowley. I recognized him, too.'

'What is his name?'

'I know him only as Yudasthir, an

Apache name for one who never gives up in battle. I also know he was a sergeant of scouts at Camp Verde.'

Dutch raised an eyebrow. 'Camp Verde?'

'That is correct. If you need to know his name, ask Al Sieber.'

'I can do that,' Dutch said. 'Do you have any idea where he is now?'

Walker smoked the Old Glory down to his fingertips, then snubbed it out. 'I hear he is with the Jicarilla Apaches,' he said.

8

A touch on my arm woke me. I reacted instantly, leaping to my feet and grasping a hand in a Cheyenne hold that could easily break its bones.

'Mister? Wilder!' Blessing was on her knees, her right hand clamped in mine. 'You're hurting me.'

I released the hold. 'Never touch me when I'm sleeping,' I said, trying to make my tone gentle. 'A man like me feels that whoever touches him when he sleeps is after a life or a scalp, maybe both. It's a habit that keeps me alive. Remember that.'

'I will remember,' she said in a tiny voice. She massaged the hand I could have torn from her arm.

'Why did you wake me?'

'When the sun rises above the eastern mountains, you must fight. I thought perhaps you might want some time to

116

prepare,' she said, her voice still soft and small.

'Prepare?'

'Do you not pray to God or *Usen* or whatever Cheyenne call the Great Spirit? Do you not meditate to make yourself ready to die?' Blessing sounded almighty concerned about one who was not of her tribe.

'A Dog Soldier must always be ready to fight,' I said, 'and so be ready to die. When I lived in Black Kettle's village, I hoped to be a Dog Soldier. I still try to be, although there are no more Dog Soldiers.'

She started to put a hand on my arm, but stopped it an inch or so away. Then she withdrew her hand. 'I am sorry,' she said.

'It was not your doing.'

She looked up, her eyes brimming. 'The pain in your heart gives me pain in mine.'

I turned to search her face, but she'd ducked her head and now stared at the ground. I changed the subject.

'Now that you have kindly wakened me, what is the chance of something to eat?' I spoke as if I were light-hearted and without care. I smiled when she glanced my way, and raised my eyebrows to emphasize the question.

Her mouth quivered with the beginnings of a smile. 'I'll see what my mother has,' she said, and left the wickiup a bit faster than usual.

I wondered what kind of knife Puma would give me to fight his son. The boy would certainly use my Bowie, which almost had a life of its own. I sat cross-legged before the fire-pit with my hands on my knees and my back straight as an iron rod. I closed my eyes and imagined the Circle of the Knife. I brought the boy Gosheven into my mind. I watched my memories of him, the way he moved, what he watched, the speed of his reactions, the accuracy of his actions, and his judgement. I watched him in my mind again and again until I felt I knew him as well as possible considering our short time on the trail.

Blessing returned with a pinole gruel. 'My mother says game is scarce. She asks you to forgive her treatment of such an honored guest.'

'I don't feel like a guest,' I said.

'Oh, but you are. Really. My father is very honored to have Yudasthir at his rancheria. He says you never give up. He says you will teach his warriors how to face death.'

I frowned. 'I don't plan to die.'

'Yes, but you must face the possibility of death soon. My father promised to treat you as an honored guest as the contest begins.' Blessing's eyes were large in the cool grey of early morning. They said she believed what she told me. Her face shone with anticipation, and I wondered if she wanted to see me die.

I ate the pinole. I needed whatever strength it would give me. The arrow channel through my back muscles burned. The headache was gone, but then, I've always been hard-headed. Four days in moccasins had just about fixed my rock-nicked feet.

A drumbeat began at the western edge of the rancheria. A single male voice chanted to the beat. Puma's people gathered slowly, turning to follow the lone drummer as he made his way through the village toward the new wickiup Blessing had raised in the shadow of the eastern mountains.

Yana he yana he ah ah hey yana hey.

A chant usually had people dancing in a rythmic shuffle-step. Not this time. The villagers simply followed the old man with the drum as he chanted.

Yana he yana he ah ah hey yana hey.

As he approached Blessing's wickiup, the crowd behind him spread out and surrounded us. The old man stopped his drumming and chanting, and sat down, cross-legged, with his back to the wickiup entrance.

Across the circle, the villagers parted and Puma walked through them in his finest buckskins.

Puma sat opposite the old man. I had no idea what to do, so I just stood there.

'Gosheven. Yudasthir.' Puma called out our names. Gosheven stepped from among the onlookers. I didn't move.

Puma gestured for Gosheven to sit at his right and me at his left. When we were positioned to his satisfaction, Puma nodded to the old man. 'Hodentin, our medicine man, will pray to *Usen* and the spirits of the mountains, who watch over the Circle of the Knife this day.'

Hodentin began a new rhythm on his hand drum. Again, no one joined in. He chanted for a moment, then lay the drum aside, stood, and turned to face the mountains. He reached into a pouch suspended from his neck by a leather thong and withdrew a pinch of yellow thule pollen, which he scattered to the four winds. 'O *Usen*, father of the six tribes. O spirits of the mountains, who protect us in our wickiups. O Earth Mother, from whom we were born and to whom we belong. Hear me. Hear me. Hear me.'

He took three steps and stopped before Gosheven. The medicine man used his right thumb to mark the boy's forehead with yellow pollen. Then he turned to me and did the same.

'O spirits who hear my voice, look upon two warrior men, two who would enter the Circle of the Knife on this sacred day. Strengthen their sinews. Strengthen their hearts. Strengthen their minds. O spirits, show these men who strive for blood that all men are brothers. Keep this place holy, O spirits of the mountain. Keep this place free of blood lust, O Earth Mother. Great *Usen*, watch over all, that your will may be done.'

Hodentin scattered another pinch of pollen to the winds. He picked up the drum and began to beat it in the original rhythm. He chanted as he had on the way to Blessing's wickiup, but now he walked back through the village and disappeared toward the west.

Slowly the villagers dispersed until only Puma, two elders, Gosheven, and I remained in the little clearing. Blessing had gone into the wickiup. 'Gosheven. Yudasthir. The sun will soon rise above the mountains. It is time. You will be at the Circle dressed in breechclout and moccasins. Bring your knives.'

'As you command, my chief,' I said, for being accepted as a guest in an Apache rancheria made me an adopted member of the tribe.

Gosheven merely rose and strode away. He was an angry young man, and anger can cause a fighter to make mistakes.

'You have no weapons, Yudasthir,' Puma said. He took a knife in a lacquered sheath from a bag that hung by a strap across his chest. 'Take this. My father brought it back from a raid against the Nakai-ye Mexicans when I was a boy. It has good medicine.'

Hesitating a moment, I accepted the knife. I turned it in my hands. The black lacquered sheath showed cracks from age, but the scrolled locket and chape shone with soft luster. The leather that wrapped the grip was too fresh to be the original, but nicks and scratches on the pommel, a large silver ball, looked like the results of fighting.

I drew the knife from its sheath. A scroll ran down the center of the double-edged blade, weaving in and out through letters that spelled Toledo. It looked to be about the same length as my Bowie, but not as heavy. The steel was gunmetal dark with a silvery edge that indicated careful whetting. I tested it on my arm, shaving a square inch of hair as quick and smooth as a barber's razor. I resheathed the Spanish blade and held it out to Puma. 'This blade should be used by someone noble born,' I said. 'It is a weapon for chiefs. I am not worthy of it.'

He held up both hands, palms out. 'Few knives match the Bowie Gosheven took from you. I would not have the great Yudasthir face his own knife across the Circle with a lesser blade.'

Puma wouldn't take the Toledo dagger back, so I kept it. And I began to form an idea, a strategy for the coming contest — to me it was a contest, not a fight. I had no grudge against Puma's son. I hefted the Toledo in its ornate sheath. I felt a tiny smile pull at the corners of my mouth.

'We await you at the Circle,' Puma said. He got to his feet slowly, as if his age were at fault. Immediately the elders stood. Puma straightened, raised his eyes to the mountains behind us, then turned and walked with inborn dignity toward the center of the village, the elders two steps behind.

'Wilder?' Blessing's voice broke into my thoughts. 'Time to get ready. The sun's almost up.' She held out an Apache breechclout.

'You always have what I need,' I said, and was surprised to see Blessing blush.

In the wickiup, I stripped, affixed the breechclout, then stepped outside. 'Wait a minute,' Blessing said, and slathered a salve of some kind on the

125

arrow wounds. Together, we walked to the Circle of the Knife, which was marked on a patch of sandy flat ground on the southwest edge of the village. I could feel my heart begin to beat faster. I took deep breaths. My eyesight sharpened. I ceased to feel the stretch and pain of the arrow wounds. My strategy meant a huge gamble. *Usen* only knew if it would succeed.

An elder positioned us, Gosheven to Puma's right, me to his left. The chief sat with his face to the sun as it topped the mountains.

I held the Spanish dagger, still sheathed, in my left hand. Gosheven had the Bowie, its blade bared, in his right, ready for blood. I turned to Puma. 'My Chief. May I say something before the contest begins?'

Puma raised his arm four square, fingers spread. 'We hear the words of Yudasthir,' he said. The villagers pressed closer.

I laid the Spanish dagger on the ground at the edge of the circle. My hands empty, I spoke to Puma, but I hoped Gosheven and the warriors of the village listened. 'Gosheven proved himself a warrior worthy of respect. His arrow drank my blood. His club put me to the ground. By right, he owns the great knife I always carried. By right, he owns the rifle that shoots eagles from the skies. Gosheven is a warrior.' I paused. Every villager watched me as if I were performing some kind of magic.

'But Gosheven is young. He has much to learn. Surely his vision quest will give him great power, as did mine.'

I had spent almost a dozen years with Al Sieber's scouts at Camp Verde and San Carlos. In an army camp, one-on-one fighting gets to levels far beyond saloon brawls. Pierre Babineau taught me savate. Lieutenant Daniels gave me lessons in boxing and wrestling, like the cadets learn at West Point. All young Gosheven knew was rough and tumble Apache style. 'I have no reason to wish for Gosheven's blood,' I said. 'Yet I must subdue him. My Cheyenne fathers demand it.'

A murmur coursed through the crowd of villagers. They could not imagine what I'd do. Blessing stood at the outer edge of the crowd as if she were afraid to watch but had to know what was going on.

'I face Gosheven with my hands bare,' I said. '*Usen* decide this day.'

I stepped to the center of the Circle and held out my left arm. 'I am ready,' I said.

Gosheven came to stand facing me, a question in his eyes and the Bowie held loosely yet competently in his right hand. He, too, offered his left arm.

The elder tied a three-foot length of plaited rawhide to my arm and then to Gosheven's. 'No warrior may cut the tether that binds,' he intoned, and stepped away. The contest in the Circle of the Knife began.

I expected wary circling, some testing of opponent strength, some glaring and posturing, but Gosheven came in a rush, the Bowie held low, cutting edge up. I barely had time to block his thrust with a forearm. I drove a right fist into his face, first two knuckles connecting solidly just below his eye. His head rocked back and the Bowie's point dropped. Gosheven staggered. I followed through, pulling him forward by the tether and smashing my right elbow into the flat of his jaw.

'Gosheven,' I said, my voice pitched for his ears only. 'You cannot beat me. I have fought too many fights. But this I promise. When we are finished. After the Circle. I swear. I will teach you how to do what I have done.'

Anger and pride flashed in Gosheven's eyes. The left one had a large mouse growing beneath it. He whipped the Bowie in a lateral sweep. I leaned back from the waist, but still the tip of the knife sliced across my chest, leaving a six-inch cut that instantly wept blood.

'And what are you going to teach me?' Gosheven said through clenched teeth. ' 'Breed.'

Anger flashed through my mind, but

I thrust it aside. I must stay cold and alert to best Gosheven and the big Bowie.

I whirled, drawing his left arm off center as my body action jerked at the tether. The force of my turning body added to the power of my clenched fist as it crashed into the left side of his face.

He staggered.

I whipped around to face him, one leg raised, bent at the knee.

Gosheven straightened, barely gaining his balance when my right foot, swinging upward in a whipping savate kick, smacked into his neck with a solid thunk.

Again he staggered, then crouched, a wounded mountain lion.

I faced him, legs apart, knees flexed, wary of his youthful strength and native Apache will to survive. The rules of the Circle forbade cutting the tethered arm. I hoped he would remember that.

Gosheven snarled and crouched low, almost to the ground. He sprang, not forward, but upward. His leap took him over my shoulder. The blade of the Bowie sought my throat, but I shifted and dropped to one knee. Still, the knife dragged across the top of my shoulder, slicing into the muscle near the base of my neck. Blood flowed to join that from the earlier cut. Both injuries were hardly more than scratches. Both looked frightful because of the blood.

Time slowed. Gosheven flew on past me, curling his body into a ball to take the shock of impact with the ground. I pulled hard on the tether to upset his balance. He sprawled when he hit, and in an instant I had him in a triangle choke hold, one of the wrestling tricks the Looie taught me. I dragged him to his feet. He kicked and flailed, but couldn't break away. With my mouth at his ear, I said, 'Gosheven. I can kill you, or save you. Are you willing to call the contest finished?'

His only answer was renewed effort to escape the hold. I kept him off balance and, strong as he was, he couldn't overpower me. I tightened the choke-hold, cutting off the blood flowing through his neck. A few seconds later, he collapsed, unconscious. I kept the tight hold for a few breaths longer, then let him fall to the ground.

I picked up the Bowie.

The villagers gasped and seemed to lean forward, anxious to see me kill the boy.

Instead, I cut the thongs that held the tether to my wrist. I walked over to Puma. 'Your son is a worthy warrior, my Chief, but he has much to learn.' I dropped the Bowie knife beside the Spanish dagger and walked away from the Circle. Blessing soon caught up with me, and we walked side by side to her wickiup.

The villagers left us alone through the day. I don't remember what we talked about because my mind was on young Gosheven.

At dusk, a lone man leading a horse walked through the village, a rifle held aslant in the crook of his arm. I could soon recognize both — Gosheven and Zeeb.

Gosheven stopped outside the clearing in front of Blessing's wickiup. 'Yudasthir. Lolotea. I would approach your wickiup.'

Blessing stood. 'You are welcome, Gosheven, son of Puma,' she said.

Gosheven inclined his head and stepped across the clearing to stand before me as I sat cross-legged on the ground.

First, he laid the one-in-a-thousand Winchester down in front of me. Then the Bowie in its hard leather sheath. And then he held out the lead rope attached to Zeeb's neck. The horse wore his saddle with its saddlebags, and his bridle. 'I return what is yours,' Gosheven said.

I waited, sensing he had more to say.

'In the Circle, you said you would teach me all you know,' Gosheven said. 'I have come to learn.'

9

Gosheven's eyes were clear, with none of the smoldering anger that had filled them before. I had promised, and a man should keep his promises. 'It's a hard road, Gosheven,' I said.

'Teach me.'

'White men and black men and Nakai-ye will soon fill the land, but it is the white man's law that will decide how we must live.'

Gosheven's face remained solemn, unmoving, trusting. He nodded.

'We will soon be unable to walk the way of the warrior,' I said. 'You and I must make our way among the white men.'

Gosheven stared at the ground. Then he looked into my eyes. 'Keep your promise, Yudasthir. Teach me.'

I started talking about something else. 'You will need help. Go once more on a vision quest. Come to me after the spirits have spoken.'

'My father says the same thing.'

'Your father is wise.'

'When the spirits have spoken, how will I know where you are, my teacher?'

I started. I'd been called a lot of things over the years, but never teacher. A weight settled on my shoulders. I took a deep breath. 'When the spirits have spoken, come to Cherry Creek in the place the whites call Tonto Basin. I will be there, building a place where I can grow old.'

Gosheven said, 'I will come.'

I picked up the Bowie and stood. 'Take this knife,' I said. 'It will remind you of the things you have learned today and protect you when evildoers seek your life. My heart is part of this knife and will always be with you.'

The boy accepted the Bowie as if it were some kind of sacred artefact. 'As my father kept the knife of the Nakaiye, handed down from his father, so I shall make this one my treasure, some day to give to my own son.'

That was the longest speech I'd ever heard Gosheven make. 'I'll be on Cherry Creek,' I said. 'Depend on it. Now go. Prepare for your vision quest.'

I sat down again as Gosheven left, and stayed there, thinking, until the skies had darkened. Blessing had watched the Fowleys ride toward La Paz, so I didn't pay any mind to them. I knew where I wanted to set up my ranch, and the title to the land could only be bought at the Gila County seat at Globe City. I'd stop there first on my way home.

Zeeb shoved at my shoulder with his muzzle. Reckon he wanted to be staked out where the grass grew belly high. He'd have to make do with short grama instead. 'Come on, Zeeb,' I said. I led him to the side of the wickiup and took off his saddle and bridle. The right-hand pouch of the saddlebags still contained an extra shirt and a pair of socks, along with a hobble strap that kept Zeeb from straying.

I had no idea where Puma's people

kept their horses, if they had any. Many Apaches preferred to walk, and they could outlast any horse on four legs. So I led Zeeb to a stand of grama grass on the eastern edge of the valley, not far from Blessing's wickiup. I hobbled him and he went to cropping the grass. 'Good to have you back, old man,' I said to the brindle dun. 'Come morning, we'll be on our way.' I still hadn't decided what to do about Blessing.

★   ★   ★

Sergeant Major Darragh Regan stared at the telegram the signal lieutenant handed him. No one ever sent him a telegram. He opened the yellow paper and read the message.

PAS SCOUT YUDASTHIR SERVED W SIEBER STOP NEED NAME STOP DO YOU KNOW STOP DUTCH

Yudasthir
Regan's thoughts went back to a

137

narrow canyon in the Chiricahua Mountains. Cochise made his peace with Tom Jeffords in '73, but Nana, Chatto, Geronimo, and other war chiefs still roamed free. Apache bands raided into Mexico and sometimes hit ranches on the American side as well.

On that hot day the second platoon of Company D pursued Nana and his warriors. The company, under command of Captain Randolf Simmons, were bivouacked at Apache Pass when a survivor staggered in, babbling of an attack on San Angelo ranch.

'They hit us just after daylight,' the man said, flinching as the stationmaster's wife applied cactus salve to his lacerations. 'Masai, it was. I recognized his red war coat. All dead but me.'

'My company must continue in pursuit of Nana,' Captain Simmons said, 'but I shall send Lieutenant Fitzgerald with a detachment to San Angelo.'

The captain pulled Sergeant-Major Regan aside. 'Go with young Fitzgerald,

Sarn't-Major. Keep him out of trouble.'

'Yes, sir. We'll need scouts, sir.'

'Take two.'

'Any two, sir?'

'Take your pick, Sarn't Major, but make it look like the lieutenant's decision.' The captain strode away, shouting as he walked: 'D Company, saddle up. We've got miles to ride before the sun goes down. Lieutenant Fitzgerald, you'll take the second platoon to San Angelo ranch. Sergeant-Major Regan will accompany you. Take two of the scouts.'

Butterfield's Apache Pass station erupted into cacophony as men and beasts prepared for the trail.

'Shall I gather the men, sir?' Regan said to Fitzgerald.

'Shit,' Fitzgerald said.

'Sir?'

'By the good lord, Sergeant-Major. Shunted off on some detail to bury dead civilians on some god-forsaken cholla-ridden ranch.'

'If it was Masai, sir, we'd best ride

with our eyes wide open,' Regan said. 'Captain said we could choose two scouts, sir. May I suggest, sir? I know them somewhat better than yourself, sir.'

'As you will,' Fitzgerald said.

Regan took the lieutenant's offhand comment as orders to organize the detachment. As scouts, he selected Wilder and Begay. Wilder was half-Cheyenne and had been raised in Black Kettle's village. Begay was Navajo, blood enemy to Apaches.

Fitzgerald's detachment rode south by twos, the lieutenant in the lead, followed by Regan, Corporal Dillenty, and eight troopers. Wilder and Begay ranged ahead, marking the trail.

San Angelo ranch lay so close to the border that it could easily be mistaken for Mexican. *Perhaps that's why Masai attacked*, Regan thought. *If Apaches hate anyone, they hate Mexicans — Nakai-ye.*

Fitzgerald and his men found nine bodies at San Angelo, six men and three women. The Apaches hadn't stopped to mutilate them. As the men dug graves, Fitzgerald paced in the shadow of the overhanging porch roof.

Regan approached the officer, stopping a respectful distance away.

'What is it?'

'All the dead bodies are adults, sir,' Regan said.

'So?'

'Pete Stoudmire had a daughter, sir.'

'Have your scouts find her,' the lieutenant said.

Regan saluted. 'Very good, sir.'

Wilder and Begay began their search, but rode back before an hour had passed. Regan reported to the lieutenant. 'Mr Fitzgerald, sir, the scouts say there's no doubt the Apaches rode off with the girl.'

Fitzgerald's eyes took on a sharp gleam. 'Get the men ready,' he said. 'We'll get that girl back.'

Regan stopped short. The detachment had two days' rations and twenty rounds of ammunition for their trapdoor Springfields. Fitzgerald and Regan had twenty .45 cartridges in their pouches and five rounds in their converted baby Dragoon revolvers. 'Pursuit, sir?' he said.

'You heard me.'

'Short rations, sir. Short on ammo, too.'

'Make do, Sergeant-Major. This is the Army.' The lieutenant stared north toward the Chiricahua Mountains. He pulled a watch from his breast pocket. 'Half an hour, Sarn't-Major. I want the platoon on the trail in half an hour.'

Three days put the detachment well into the Chiricahua range. Regan put the soldiers on half-rations when the platoon left San Angelo. The scouts lived off the land.

'Scout signal, sir,' Regan said.

'I see him,' the lieutenant said, and held up his hand to stop the troops.

Wilder and Begay walked their horses onto the trail from behind a boulder the size of a mountain cabin. Wilder spoke to Regan. 'Ambush spot ahead, *ma'hahkeso*.'

'You'll make your reports to me, Wilder,' Fitzgerald snapped.

Wilder stopped talking.

'Well?'

Wilder looked at Regan, an eyebrow raised.

'Report, son,' Regan said.

Wilder nodded. 'Land spreads out through the cut, Lieutenant,' he said. 'High ground on both sides. If I was Masai, that's where I'd hit a little bunch like ours.'

'Is that it?'

Wilder looked at Regan, then back at Fitzgerald. 'That's all,' he said.

'Give us outriders, Sarn't Major. We'll move on and get that girl.'

Regan and Wilder shared a look. 'Evans. Richards.' Regan shouted.

'Ho-o.' Two troopers broke from the by-twos column and spurred their mounts forward.

'Mr Fitzgerald wants outriders. You're elected,' Regan said as they came abreast.

The troopers dragged out their Springfield single-shot carbines and checked the loads. They held the Springfields on their thighs like lances, and rode to positions twenty yards ahead and ten yards wide on each side of the little column.

'We'd better go first,' Wilder said to Regan. He motioned to Begay and the two scouts walked their horses toward the cut. Wilder shucked his one-of-a-kind Winchester 73, pulled a bag of bullets from his offside saddlebag and hung it around his neck. Regan had practiced with Wilder when he was just a boy, and knew few could match him as a sharpshooter. The sergeant-major avoided thinking about what waited on the other side of the cut.

'Lead out, Sarn't-Major.' Fitzgerald's voice sounded flat in the still air.

The scouts had disappeared into the cut when the column moved forward, Springfields at the ready. The out-riders went in, then the column followed. The sandy trail wound between walls of red sandstone at least fifty feet high for a hundred yards or more. Then the walls fell away and the trail divided into two.

Regan's ears picked up only the sound of iron horseshoes clipping stone as the column moved forward. No wind. No insect noise. No bird calls. He didn't like it. He pulled his baby Dragoon from its holster and cocked the hammer.

The land rose slightly between the two trails, and the walls of the cut had become jumbles of sandstone thrown hither and yon by eons of wind, rain, and possibly the shaking of the earth.

Evans took the left-hand trail and Richards took the right. The scouts were out of sight. Two *zopilote* buzzards circled high in the cloudless sky. Regan sweated, though the day was cool by southern Arizona standards.

Lieutenant Fitzgerald chose to ride after Evans, and the platoon followed.

Four Apaches erupted from the very sand of the trail. Two were astride the outriders' horses before the troopers could react. Evans and Richards fell, throats slashed to the bone. They kicked and thrashed until the desert sand had drunk all their blood. Their attackers spurred the cavalry mounts up into the tumbled boulders of the high ground.

Lieutenant Fitzgerald met his assailant with a doubled fist that knocked the warrior to the ground. Instead of fumbling at the Dragoon in its flapped holster, Fitzgerald drew the saber that hung from his McClellan saddle and stabbed it through the Apache. An arrow sprouted from the lieutenant's back, and he barely managed to stay in the saddle. The wounded Apache staggered into the sandstone jumble.

The fourth warrior aimed for Regan, leaping high to swing his war club. Regan shoved the Dragoon in the Apache's face and pulled the trigger. A mist of red hung in the air for a moment after the attacker fell away.

'To the high ground,' Regan yelled, and spurred his horse up the small rise between the trails. The lieutenant's horse went down, and shots from the heights registered on Regan's mind. Then his horse stumbled, stood for a few seconds wagging its head from side to side, then fell to its knees and over onto its side. Regan stepped out of the saddle as the horse rolled. It heaved a sigh and went still.

'Dismount and fire at will!' Regan dropped behind the body of his mount and scanned the jumbled sandstone heights across the trail.

Regan saw no cover worth the word where he and the troopers grouped. 'Put the horses down,' he shouted. 'Give us some cover.' Shots rang out as the cavalrymen killed their horses; their bodies would give the men the only protection they could hope for.

'Situation, Corporal?'

'Bradford's nicked in the foot, Sarn't-Major. Others is OK.'

'Keep an eye out. Shoot only at what you can see. Don't waste cartridges.'

'Yo.' Corporal Dillenty spread the word.

Lieutenant Fitzgerald lay behind his

dead horse. Regan couldn't tell if he was alive or dead, but he had no doubt the Apaches would not leave Fitzgerald be.

Puffs of smoke lifted from the sandstone heights. Cracks of Springfield rifle fire followed. The platoon answered in kind. Then Regan heard the sound of a running horse, and Wilder's grulla pony thundered into sight, Wilder himself hung by a heel and a handhold, firing his Winchester from beneath the pony's neck. As the horse approached Fitzgerald's dead mount, Wilder dropped his feet to the ground, ran for a few steps, and let go of the saddle. The pony galloped on down the trail and into the cut. Wilder stood with his feet slightly spread, facing the sandstone heights. He began to chant.

Eiya eiya haiya ha ho yey eiya haiya yaiya hoyey eiya hoya hey.

Regan had heard that chant before, and recognized it as a Cheyenne death song.

Deliberately, Wilder fished cartridges

from the bag hanging on his neck and filled the magazine of the Winchester '73.

Eiya eiya haiya ha ho yey eiya haiya yaiya hoyey eiya hoya hey.

He threw the Winchester to his shoulder and snapped a shot at the heights. An Apache fell from his perch atop a house-sized boulder. He lay motionless where he landed.

Puffs of smoke answered Wilder's shot. Wilder sang his death song. None of the Apache bullets hit him. He picked another target and a second warrior fell lifeless to the ground. Wilder's chant climbed to a higher pitch and greater volume. He stood before the lieutenant's horse as if staked in place.

A third brave fell to Wilder's Winchester. And a fourth.

Then the killing field fell silent, except for Wilder's chant. No movement in the heights. No puffs of rifle smoke. The *zopilotes* circled lower, intent on the dead horses.

'*Ma'hahkeso*,' Wilder called.

'I hear you,' Regan said, 'and don't call me 'old man'.'

'Masai is gone. He'll not be back. The fight cost too much.' Wilder leaned his Winchester against the lieutenant's dead horse and knelt by the sprawled officer. 'The lieutenant breathes,' he said.

'Keep your eyes peeled,' Regan said to the soldiers. 'Those Apaches may not be gone.' He went to check on the lieutenant. As Wilder said, he was alive.

Wilder had sent Begay to Captain Simmons, and Company D found the second platoon three days later. The dead horses had provided two days' rations before the meat went bad, and Wilder had fed the men with cottontails and pack rats and prickly pears after that. The lieutenant rode Wilder's grulla pony.

After they returned to San Carlos, the soldiers often told the story of Wilder and his death song. The Apaches began to call him Yudasthir, and the Army gave him a Medal of Honor.

10

'Mister? Wilder?' Blessing's voice was low and tentative. I looked at her in answer.

She held the money belt. 'The fight is over,' she said. 'I return what is yours.' She spoke to me in English, but her words echoed the rhythm of Apache. 'What will you do now?'

'I'll be going to Globe City,' I said. 'There's a spring feeding Cherry Creek on the Tonto that I'll buy with some of the gold.'

She placed the belt on the ground in front of me. Without another word she turned and went back into the wickiup.

Time to hit the trail. I took the bridle and went for Zeeb. When I led him back, the wickiup was on fire and Blessing was gone.

I saddled Zeeb, and couldn't help wondering what Blessing was up to. No telling with a woman. I gave up. The bag of coffee beans was still in the saddlebags. My two canteens had been returned, too. I planned to fill them at the seep on the way out of the village. Mentally, I mapped my course as I prepared to leave. I'd go to Wickenburg first, where I'd get a new Bowie, then to Crown King. Follow Cave Creek to Red Mountain, and cut across the desert to the foothills of the Superstitions. I wondered if prospectors still searched for the lost mine they said was up around the Weaver's Needle.

Past the west end of the Superstitions, I'd go on towards Florence until I could see Picketpost Mountain in the east. Then I would cut through the badlands to Globe City. In a week's time I'd have title to my little valley off Cherry Creek.

Zeeb and I walked through the village to Puma's wickiup. His wife greeted me with a bowl of pinole. 'Yudasthir. You must have this before you leave us,' she said. She offered me the wooden bowl.

I took it and squatted by the fire-pit. A tendril of smoke rose from the coals. Puma did not appear until I'd eaten the pinole and returned the bowl. 'You will leave us then, Yudasthir?' he said.

I'd not seen or heard him approach, not that I'd been listening. Still, it bothered me that he could do it. 'Yes, my Chief. I must continue. I seek a place in which to grow old. Some day I wish for sons as stalwart as those of Puma.'

The chief sat to my right. 'You may need protection where you go,' he said. 'Hodentin prepared this medicine pouch for you.' He handed me a doeskin pouch on a leather thong. I slipped it over my head. It felt right.

I bowed my head to Puma, expressing my thanks with silence, then rose and mounted Zeeb. 'May *Usen* protect you,' I said.

'We are always your family, Yudasthir.'

I rode for Wickenburg.

Reed Fowley lounged at his customary table at the back of the Black Diamond. He tossed down his third shot of Redbreast, Irish whiskey brought from the old country. The warm heat in his belly and the pleasant tingling in his crotch where Tillie Mae had spent a good thirty minutes sucking him dry brought a smile of satisfaction to his face. *What a life*. Reed's smile widened. His eyes swept the room.

Paddy O'Hara stood behind the bar like a solid block of oak. Red Schiendist sat the high stool with a sawed-off double gun across his knees. Big Ben Wheelwright looked half asleep where he stood against the back wall, but Reed knew he would as soon break a man in two across his knee as kiss one of the whores.

Whores.

Hot damn but they were good to have around the place. A man in Reed's position, a man who was as good as owner of the Black Diamond, could pick and choose; which he did often, sometimes twice a day.

Ah Choy, the Chinaman cook, put out the saloon's free lunch. Thick slices of white wheat bread. Two pots of butter. A plate mounded high with sliced ham. Another of turkey slices. Dill pickles in a barrel. Roast beef. The Black Diamond laid out a good lunch, but for the most part those who ate drank a lot more than the cost of their food. Mostly.

Reed gulped another shot of Redbreast.

A man pushed the doors of the Black Diamond inward as he entered. He looked familiar to Reed, but then, many men in Ehrenburg looked familiar. Reed poured another shot of whiskey into his glass. The place behind his eyes was beginning to buzz, and he savored the sensation. He ruled the Black Diamond, and when the old man died, he'd rule the town. He looked up from his dream of the future to find the man standing in front of him, hat in hand.

'Mr Fowley,' the man said, 'you don't know me. I'm Mel Garfield. I met your father at Adam's Well. I've got a whore to sell you.'

Reed perked up. New stuff. He heard of Garfield and his two women. 'Which one ya selling?'

Garfield sidled toward the food on the plank-on-barrels table at the end of the bar. He licked his lips, then shifted his gaze back to Reed.

'Hungry?' Reed had a smile on his face that never came close to his eyes. 'We agree on a price, and you're welcome to all you can eat, first drink on the house.'

The pimp sidled a little closer to the food. 'She'd be cheap at a hundred,' he said. 'Polly'd make you more than that in a day.'

'Then why ya selling?'

'Fare to Frisco,' Garfield said. 'I'm not cut out for this country. I like to died out there in that desert.'

'Give you fifty. That's fare to Frisco

and change. Stage leaves every morning.'

Garfield nodded. 'Done,' he said, and started for the food.

'Whoa up, there,' Reed said. 'Bring the bitch in first, then eat.'

With a longing look at the stacks of meat and bread, Garfield left the Black Diamond.

Reed quaffed another two fingers of Redbreast. He felt warm and good and confident. He'd just added to the Black Diamond's assets for a pittance. Pa'd be happy about that. It was hard to make Pa happy. Reed succeeded only rarely. In fact, Pa had threatened to take the Black Diamond away from Reed if he didn't straighten up and run the saloon like a business. Reed frowned. What good was it to own a saloon if a man couldn't drink when he wanted and poke a whore at will? Damn Thad had added on to his Play Pen, hung chandeliers, brought in traveling shows with singers and dancers and even actors that quoted that English dude,

157

Shakespeare. Reed wondered where his brother got the money, and why the Play Pen was always full of laughing people when the Black Diamond had maybe two poker games going and five or six men against the bar. Reed considered his whores, five in all, but they got maybe one go-round upstairs in a night. Shit.

Except for the Mexican cantina down by the river, all the saloons in Ehrenburg were owned by a Fowley, so brother competed against brother, and father against son.

Garfield burst into the Black Diamond with Polly in tow, fighting and howling. 'Asshole!' she hollered. 'You don't own me. I ain't no nigger slave. You promised we'd make a place together. You promised!'

'Here's Polly,' Garfield said. 'Where's my fifty?'

'Bring her to the office,' Reed said. He left his bottle and glass on the table and walked to what he called his office. It was more like a storeroom, but did have a couple of chairs and a small table.

Garfield dragged Polly to the room, his face deadpan.

Reed unlocked the cashbox that was chained to the floor and took out two double eagles and a single. He handed the money to Garfield with his right hand and clamped a hard grip on Polly's arm with his left. 'Enjoy your meal,' he said.

The door closed behind Garfield and Polly screamed the high wail of a scorned woman left behind. She jerked at Reed's grip, then scratched at him with bared nails. He casually back-handed her across the face. Her scream stopped as if cut off by a sharp razor. Reed hit her from the other side. Her knees sagged. Blood dribbled from her nose. Both sides of her face showed red welts from Reed's hard fingers. She drooled from the corner of her mouth and her eyes glazed.

Reed smacked her again with a big open hand. 'You're mine, bitch. Body and soul, what little you have.' He opened a small door in the back of the room and shoved her through it. 'We'll see how uppity you are when I get back,' he said, and locked the door with a large key he took from a hook on the wall. He grinned. Another one to tame. He licked his lips.

Garfield stood at the end of the lunch slab, wolfing food with both hands.

'Draw me a beer,' Reed said to Paddy. When he came back with a mug dripping foam, Reed took it over to Garfield. 'You'll want something to wash that good grub down,' he said, and handed him the mug.

Garfield nodded his thanks, both cheeks bulged so he looked like a squirrel putting away its winter store of acorns. He sipped at the beer and used it to wash the chewed mass of ham and bread and butter down his throat. 'Obliged,' he said.

Reed went back to the table where he'd left his bottle of Redbreast. He poured a generous three fingers and gulped the whiskey down in as many swallows. The glow warmed up again. He thought about the whore named Polly. He'd see how pliant a slave she was.

The setting of the sun saw Reed with an empty bottle and an almost empty saloon. Once in a while a whore would come to the second-floor balcony and look at the crowd. With hardly anyone drinking, the girls stayed upstairs. Damn. Reed could hear a tinkle of music and laughter from the Play Pen down the street. Damn. He had booze. He had women. He had a fairly clean card game. What in hell was keeping people away from his saloon?

The front door swung open and three men Reed didn't know came in. His eyes brightened. Sheep to fleece, if he was lucky. Two whores clattered down the stairs and simpered their way toward the men, who ignored them.

Reed watched the men from beneath furrowed brows. They appeared casual enough, yet there was a tension about them. He couldn't put a finger on what bothered him. He broke the seal on a new bottle of Redbreast, uncorked it, and splashed a generous portion into his glass. He'd planned to sip the whiskey, but ended up taking a mouthful.

The men now stood with their elbows hooked on the bar, a glass of house whiskey in their left hands. They looked straight at Reed. The smallest of the three, a slim man in striped California pants and gray frock-coat, pushed away from the bar and walked over to Reed's table.

'Good evening, sir,' he said, his voice a soft Southern drawl. 'My friends and I came up river on the General Jackson. We heard the Black Diamond hosted interesting card games.' The man looked around the nearly empty saloon. 'But it appears that we heard wrong.'

Shark Benson, the Black Diamond's resident gambler, wasn't there. Maybe he'd stepped out for a piss or something. 'We sometimes get a good game going,' Reed said. 'What did you have in mind?'

'Seven-card stud,' the man said. 'My friends and I don't play penny ante though.'

Somehow Reed kept from rubbing his hands together. Sheep to fleece. Reed prided himself as one of the best poker-players in Ehrenburg. 'Our dealer's out right now,' he said, 'but if you want, I'll personally set up a table.' He stuck out his right hand. The cut from the 'breed's Bowie had healed and a slight stretching sensation was the only thing left to remind Reed of the humiliation he'd suffered. He couldn't help grimacing. 'I'm Reed Fowley, owner of the Black Diamond,' he said.

The man ignored Reed's outstretched hand. 'I'm Nathaniel Broadbent,' he said, 'and these men are Bart Wilkins and Whip Norton.'

The men at the bar nodded at Broadbent's introduction.

Reed stood, perhaps too quickly, because he needed to grip the edge of the table to steady himself. He gestured toward a round felt-topped table. 'Shall we play over there?'

'As you wish, Mr Fowley.' Broadbent beckoned to the other men. They took chairs at the table, and each placed a poke on the felt tabletop.

Broadbent smiled and nodded. Norton and Wilkins remained poker-faced.

News of the high-stakes game flashed through Ehrenburg. The Black Diamond began to fill with curious men. Reed's whores worked the crowd and made trip after trip up the stairs to the cribs. Paddy had to break open a new barrel of house whiskey. The babble became a roar, and Reed Fowley could not help smiling. This was how the Black Diamond was supposed to be.

Reed emptied the cash box of gold coins for the game, and until well after midnight he had a comfortable pile of eagles and double eagles. Sometimes the luck ran in his favor, sometimes not. Then his luck began to change for the worse. First Norton dropped out of the game, then Wilkins. Both had lost some from their pokes, but not much.

'Shall we continue, Mr Fowley?' Broadbent asked.

Reed's losses stood at slightly more than $1,000, money he could not afford. Nothing to do but keep playing. He had to win it back. 'New deck,' he called to Paddy.

The bartender brought the new cards over. 'Close up, Paddy. It's time everyone left,' Reed said. He turned to Broadbent. 'Let's take a few moments off. We'll start again at three o'clock, if that's all right with you.'

'As you wish, Mr Fowley.'

'Red. Ben. Keep an eye on the table. Mr Broadbent and I will refresh ourselves.'

Red Shiendist cocked the hammers of his sawed-off, and Big Ben came over to stand next to the table, massive arms folded but ready for instant action. Reed went to the back room.

A few minutes later, Paddy brought in the night's take. 'Not bad, sor,' he said. 'More than three thousand, drinks and whores.'

The take gave Reed a fall-back, but it was all in small coins and bills. Never mind. He put the take in the cash box, took a deep breath, and returned to the poker table.

By four o'clock Reed's pile of coins was gone. He scrubbed a hand across the stubble that now covered his jaw. Eyes closed, he reached for the bottle of Redbreast. A drink. That's what he needed, a drink.

'Mr Fowley? What do you think? Would you like a chance to recover what you lost?'

Reed's head jerked around. Win back his gold? He gulped at the whiskey and ignored the alarm bell in his brain. 'How?' he asked.

Broadbent leaned across the table and spoke in a soft drawl that carried only as far as Reed Fowley's ears. 'I have somewhat more than five thousand dollars on the table here, Mr Fowley. I propose you do one of two things. Your choice.'

Reed kept his eyes on Broadbent's face as he took another slug of Redbreast, emptying his glass. He poured more and noticed the bottle was nearly empty, but Broadbent was about to tell him how to get his money back. He ignored the low level in the bottle and once more concentrated on Broadbent.

'I see two possible outcomes,' Broadbent said. 'One, you sign a quit claim to the Black Diamond, I give you five thousand dollars, and you take whatever cash there is in the office. With that money, you could hunt down the half-breed who nearly destroyed you and get rid of him once and for all.'

'How'd you hear about the 'breed?'

'Everyone west of Santa Fe knows of the 'breed and how the Fowleys have been eating humble pie because of him.'

The space behind Reed's eyes began to burn. The 'breed. The reason for all his bad luck. His right hand clenched.

He was strong again. He could take the 'breed. But wait. 'What's the other thing?' he asked.

'There used to be a couple of ranchers up on a little creek in the foothills of the White Mountains,' Broadbent said. 'Marion Clark and Corydon Cooley. I reckon they partnered for half a dozen years, but their thinking wasn't the same and they took to arguing.'

Broadbent took a tiny sip from the glass of whiskey he'd only refilled once during the night. 'Some would have settled the argument with six-guns. Cooley and Clark decided to settle their differences with a deck of cards.'

Another tiny sip.

'Here's what Cooley said. 'Show low and take the ranch.' And that's what I say to you. We'll cut the deck. If you show the low card, you win everything on the table and keep your saloon.'

Reed thought about his luck. He thought about how the Black Diamond had slid downhill. He saw the 'breed, and the scar across his right bicep itched. His eyes took in the $5,000 in gold on the table, and his mind counted nearly $4,000 in the cash box.

'I'll sign the quit claim,' he said.

11

Coming out of the Harcuvars, a man can see the smoke of Wickenburg and the green of willows and box alder and cottonwood along the Hassayampa river. The town had grown some since I was there with a company of cavalry from Camp Verde. The stage road from Ehrenburg turned into Wickenburg's main street. I stopped first at Goldwater's Emporium. My canvas shirt was the worse for wear and I'd fit in better with boots instead of knee-high moccasins. It took me only three or four minutes to buy what I needed, a couple more to change, and I walked out of Goldwater's a different man, in looks anyway.

On down the main drag toward the river, there was an eating place called Mother Lode. Henry Wickenburg named the place after the gold vein he'd found in Vulture City. I'd not had anything to eat since the pinole at Puma's rancheria, so I tethered Zeeb to the hitching rail and went in to have myself a feed.

I was just mopping up the last of the gravy with a chunk of sourdough when a man stopped at my table.

'You'll be Wilder, then?' he said.

I put the gravy-soaked bread in my mouth, chewed, and swallowed while the man watched. I took the time to once him over. A tall dark man dressed in gray from head to foot, including a flat-brimmed Stetson. He wore a Frontier Colt high on his left hip, positioned for a cross draw. He looked like he could use the gun, too.

'I'm Falan Wilder,' I said.

He smiled. 'Proud to meet you, Wilder,' he said. 'Heard of that fight with Masai's bunch over in the Chiricahuas. Thought it might be you.'

I arched an eyebrow.

He noticed my question. 'I'm Ness Havelock,' he said. 'US Marshal.'

'You looking for me?'

Havelock shook his head. 'Not me. But someone else is.'

The Fowleys, I figured, but I still asked. 'Who?'

'Ex-Pinker named Dutch Regan.'

I must have blinked at the name. 'Know him?'

I didn't answer for a moment. I couldn't figure why Dutch would want me. 'I know him,' I said. 'His folks raised me after Chivington killed Black Kettle's people at Sand Creek. Wonder why he wants to find me?'

'Haven't the slightest.' Havelock waved at my Winchester. 'That the rifle you sang your death song over?'

My turn to smile. 'Seemed like a good enough day to die. Yeah, that's it.'

'Could I have a look?'

I handed him the one-in-a-thousand Winchester. He handled it with care and didn't work the lever. 'Bet this shoots where you point it,' he said, holding the rifle out to me.

'It does.'

'Thought you were partial to a Bowie.'

'Lost mine. I'll get another.'

'Can I give you a bit of advice?'

I nodded.

'Get yourself a good short gun, too. Maybe with a long barrel. You've got a good eye, and you can't carry a rifle all the time.'

'Bowie works close in,' I said.

'But not at fifty feet. Anyway. Just a suggestion. Want me to tell Dutch I saw you?'

I shrugged. 'I got nothing to hide.'

'Sometimes things get hard for us half-breeds,' he said, and smiled. 'Half Cherokee, half Texas Ranger.'

My turn. 'Half Cheyenne and half God knows what.'

'Mind me asking where you're headed?'

'Cherry Creek,' I said. 'Got me a place all picked out. Figure to raise horses and maybe some beef.'

'Stock?'

'I mustanged up on the Paradise,' I

said. 'The McCulloughs are saving me some of the best from Big Red's herd.'

Havelock stepped back. 'Us'ns always have to ride with both eyes wide open,' he said. 'But you know that. If you ever need help, send word to me at the RP Connected outside Saint Johns, or to my brother Garet at his H-Cross ranch on Silver Creek. You need us, we'll come.'

'Obliged,' I said. 'Kinda used to skinning my own cats, but if the day ever comes . . . '

I finished a second cup of coffee after Havelock left. I'd heard of his brother Garet. He'd pulled a gun on Juanito O'Rourke when the killer had the drop on him and lived to tell the tale. Havelocks were good men to have on your side. I paid four bits for the meal and left.

Zeeb waited hipshot at the rail. He deserved a feed as much as I did, and Hartley's Livery was two blocks along, down on the river bank. We took our time, looking over the town as we went.

There it was, on the left. Alexander Smithson, Guns, Clocks, Fine Metalwork. Close enough to Hartley's for me to walk back while Zeeb ate.

'What'll it be?' Evan Hartley said.

'Hello, Ev,' I said, and he gave me a second hard look.

'Wilder? Wilder. My God. It's been a coon's age. Light'n set. Shee-it.' He took a good look at Zeeb. 'That's a gaw-dawful plug you're riding,' he said. 'Ain't never seen a brindle grulla before.'

I kept my poker face on. 'Out in the desert or up on the mountain, a body can't see Zeeb at all unless he flicks a tail or flops an ear. I like that.'

Hartley nodded. 'I can see that, knowing you. Still scouting?'

'Nah. Mustanged me a grubstake. Gonna raise horses up on Cherry Creek.' I got down off Zeeb and handed the reins to Hartley. 'Good bait of oats and all the hay he can eat. I'll be back directly.' I shucked the Winchester from its scabbard and took off up the road towards Smithson's.

That shop had more kinds of guns than I knew there were. A cowbell clanked when I opened the door and a stooped man with a fringe of graying hair running around under his bald pate came out of the back room, wiping his hands on an oily rag. ''Do for you?' he asked.

I'd thought he was an older man, but up close I saw he was no more than thirty or so.

'I had me a James Black Bowie,' I said. 'Sweet blade. Somebody else's got it now, and I thought maybe you'd have something like it.'

Smithson's pale-blue eyes sharpened. 'James Black blade, eh. He put a piece of that star in it?'

'Wouldn't know, but it sure held an edge.'

'Hmm. I got Bowie's but they ain't by James Black. Rare, those blades are.'

'Could you show me what you have? I'd like something heavy with the blade a little over a foot long.'

Smithson disappeared into the back of the shop and returned with an armload of knives, most of them in hard leather sheaths. He dumped them on the counter. 'All I got in that size of Bowie,' he said.

I took my time. The knives were well cared for and sharp, but none came close to the Bowie I'd given Gosheven. I drew a deep breath. 'Don't see what I'm looking for, Mr Smithson,' I said.

'Alex.'

'OK. Alex. These are all you have?'

For a moment he was silent. 'I do have one more,' he said slowly, as if he were reluctant to mention the knife. 'It's not a Bowie.'

'I'd like to see it, if I could.'

Smithson took the pile of Bowies back where they came from. When he returned, he had the strangest knife I'd ever seen. 'It's called a kukri,' he said.

The knife was close to a foot and a half long, hid in a black leather sheath with a brass point guard. A hardwood handle that looked like walnut stuck out of the sheath and two much smaller handles protruded to each side.

I pulled the knife out. Where a Bowie blade curves up to a point, the whole blade of this knife took a downward turn. The blade was more than a quarter of an inch thick and a little over a foot long — just what I had asked for. It balanced perfectly in my hand. 'Kukri?'

'Yeah. Kukri.'

'What kind of language is that?'

'No idea. But a man I knew was a CSA captain before he turned twenty. When the war ended, he had no place to go, and the only thing he knew was fighting, so he went where the fighting was. He died a general in some place called Assam, and his effects were sent to his sister. She didn't have use for the weapons so she sold them to me, us living in the same town and all.'

I hefted the kukri again. It felt right. 'How much?'

Smithson squinted at me, calculating. 'You seem to be a man who appreciates a good blade. Let's say twenty-five bucks.'

'Twenty-five? I could get a rifle for that much.'

'Not one like your Winchester. It cost seventy if a nickel.'

He had me. I changed the subject. 'I need a short gun, too. Nothing fancy, but something that shoots straight.'

'People shoot straight, not guns,' Smithson said with a grin. 'I reckon you shoot straighter than most.'

'The Winchester and me get along good,' I said.

'These days, people want Colt Single Action Army or Remington Army six-guns. But let me tell you this. If you want to shoot straight with a handgun, you want something heavy, with a long barrel. Getting your gun out quick, like some who call themselves shootists, won't keep you alive.' He opened a draw and pulled out two six-shooters.

'This one's a Whitneyville Dragoon Colt,' he said. 'I rebuilt it. Chambered the cylinder for cartridges. It shoots

.44–40s, and it's got a nine-inch rifled barrel.' He put the big gun down and picked up one slightly smaller.

'You won't see many of these,' he said. 'It's a Rogers and Spencer. Made in New York State somewhere, and I'll tell you, this here gun shoots straight. Made at the end of the war, but never used, they say. Hardly see any. This one's .44 caliber, and I converted it to take .44–40 shells, too, same as your rifle. The barrel's eight inches and a bit. A little short, but the gun shoots right.'

'Can I try 'em?'

'Come on out back.'

Out behind the shop, Smithson loaded the Dragoon and handed it to me. I shot at the man-sized target about fifty feet away, and managed to nick it five times out of six. Then he gave me the loaded Rogers and Spencer. I fired six shots. All took the target in the torso.

Smithson reloaded the Spencer. 'Take a shot or two at that target further out,' he said, pointing to a square board off up the hill. It had to be close to a hundred yards. 'The gun's got sights. Use them. Stand sideways to where you're going to shoot. Hold your arm straight out.'

I did what he said, and hit the target with four out of six shots. 'Gun shoots good,' I said.

Smithson looked at me deadpan. 'People shoot good, not guns,' he said again.

Back inside, I went around in front of the counter. 'Let's get serious,' I said. 'I want the Spencer and the kukri. I don't want to give two month's pay for them.'

'Give me twenty-five for the knife,' Smithson said, 'and I'll throw in the Spencer and a box of .44–40s for another ten bucks.'

'Deal,' I said. 'And give me five more boxes of .44–40s.'

'Done. Gonna start a war?' He got a black leather belt and holster from the back room. 'This goes with the Spencer,' he said.

I paid. 'Don't figure to start a war,' I

said, 'but I'll be ready if someone else starts one.'

On the way back to Hartley's Livery, Blessing crossed my mind. She'd burned the wickiup, which said she wouldn't return to Puma's rancheria. I wondered where she'd gone.

★ ★ ★

Dutch Regan met with Sean Fowley and two of his sons in the office at the Shamrock saloon. The old man looked haggard and worn, with a two-day stubble of gray on his jowls.

'Shall I wait for the other boy?' Dutch asked.

Fowley shook his head.

'My brother Reed won't be coming,' Thad said.

Dutch raised an eyebrow. 'I thought this whole ballyhoo was about him.'

'It was. It is,' the old man said. 'What do you have to tell us?'

Dutch stood up and moved back a step so he could see all three men. 'The name of the man you want is Falan Wilder. It's the name given him by his foster parents, Darragh and Fiona Regan, who gave him a home after his Cheyenne mother died under Chivington's guns at Sand Creek. No one knows what became of his father. No one cares. He joined the army at seventeen and served with General Crook's scouts. Three years ago, Apaches under Masai attacked a platoon of cavalry in the Chiricahua Mountains. The lieutenant was down and the sergeant-major and his men took cover behind the dead bodies of their own horses. Wilder sent the other scout for the main column and stood over the wounded lieutenant, singing his death song. He routed the Apaches with a single rifle. He saved my father's life and the US Army gave him the Medal of Honor.'

'Dear God,' Fowley said. 'He was just a 'breed.'

'I told you something was wrong,' Thad said. 'I told you we should forget about it.'

'Shee-it,' said Bud. 'A goldam hero.'

'US Marshal Ness Havelock told me Wilder plans to build a horse ranch on Cherry Creek in the Tonto Basin. He suggested that I leave him be. I take Ness Havelock's suggestions serious,' Dutch said.

After Dutch Regan left, the room was silent except for Sean Fowley's labored breathing.

'Shee-it. A motherless bloody hero,' Bud said again.

'Go,' Fowley said. 'It's over.'

Thad nodded. 'It is. And good riddance.' He left.

Bud scraped his chair back. 'I'll find Reed,' he said. 'I'll tell him about the half-breed hero.'

Fowley said nothing as Bud strode from the room. He hacked and coughed and spat blood into the handkerchief he always carried. When it got too bloody, he burned the evidence and broke out a new one. Meaghan was gone, and Fowley did not fear death.

Bud Fowley rode into Sweetwater just after sundown. He found it hard to believe the place actually had a name. Half a dozen tarpaper shacks. A Texas-style log cabin with a dog run. A single frame building with a weathered board painted with the words Ace High. Bud reined in at the Ace High, dismounted, and wrapped the reins to his bay twice around the single hitching rail. He worked his gunbelt around until the pistol was at his crotch with the handle to his right hand. He squared his bowler hat and pushed through the off-white door.

Inside, the Ace High was like any run-down frontier whiskey joint. A plank bar on two barrels. Three tables with rickety chairs. Rough-sawn floor. No mirror. No bottles. A one-eyed man stood behind the bar. Bud went up to him because there was no one else in the room. 'Bottle of Redbreast?' he asked.

'Got rotgut,' the barkeep said. 'Take it or leave it.'

'Take it.'

The 'keep ladled something into a tin cup and put it on the bar. 'Ain't got no glasses. All broke. Two bits.'

Bud paid his quarter and picked up the cup. He sipped and nearly gagged. 'How many rattlesnake heads?' he asked.

'Couple. Gives it a little punch.' The 'keep's grin showed several missing teeth.

'I'm looking for a man,' Bud said.

'You law?'

'Nah. He's m'brother.'

'That so?'

'Name's Reed. Reed Fowley. I heard he was headed in this direction.'

'That so?'

The front door creaked open. Bud kept his eyes on the barkeep.

'You looking for me, big brother?'

Bud turned to see a different Reed Fowley. He still looked big and sloppy, but his eyes burned with an inner fire.

His hands clenched into fists when he spoke. He wore a Remington Army, and somehow it fit. 'Howdy, Reed,' Bud said.

'You figure to take me back to face Pa?'

Bud shook his head. 'Heard you were set on paying back that 'breed for what he done to you.'

'I am. I hired a bunch men to ride with me, the best Tom Ranklin can get.'

'Tom Ranklin? Don't he have a hideout up Big Johney Gulch?'

'He does. Them hardcase men ride hard and shoot straight,' Reed said with pride in his voice.

'Got room for another?'

'Who?'

'Me. I know where the sumbitch breed is at.'

12

I should learn to stay out of saloons.
Just wanting a drink to celebrate selling
my horses and making the first step
toward a place of my own is what got
me in trouble with the Fowleys in the
first place. But after I filed for
homestead rights and bought 1,300
acres across the mouth of Lone Pine
Canyon, I felt a drink was in order. I'd
bought a lop-eared pack mule and
loaded him with necessities for building
a homestead. Naturally his name was
Lop Ear, and I tied his lead rope
alongside Zeeb's reins at the hitching
rail in front of the Copper King. One
shot of rye whiskey and we'd hit the
trail up Salt River to Cherry Creek and
on to Lone Pine Canyon. That's what I
thought.

Globe City's not a hot place, up off
the desert like it is, and inside the

Copper King, where it's dark and still, I felt downright cool. I carried my Winchester, the Spencer rode just behind my right hip, and I'd done some work on the kukri sheath so it sat just right in the small of my back. Its hardwood handle was where I'd naturally reach for it.

At the end of the bar, I pushed my Stetson back on my head, leaned the Winchester against the wall, and signalled to the barkeep, who was buffing glasses to a shine at the other end of the bar. He finished the polishing job and sauntered over to where I stood.

'The Copper King serves only gentlemen,' he said. 'It's also against the law to sell liquor to Indians.'

I smiled. 'My name's Falan Wilder,' I said. 'I own the Flying W outfit.'

'Never heard of a Flying W in these parts.'

'You will.' I paused a moment. 'How about a shot of rye?' I laid a double eagle on the bar.

'Don't stock rye whiskey,' the bar-keep said.

'Turley's Mill?'

He shook his head.

'Old Potrero?'

'Can't sell liquor to Indians.'

He was polite. He never told me to get out or get my stinking paws off his polished bar. He just wouldn't sell me the time of day. 'I wonder,' I said, 'if my friend Ness Havelock, you know, the US marshal, if he was to come in, would you be able to find some whiskey to serve him?'

The barkeep looked uncomfortable.

'Havelock's half Cherokee, you know. Like I'm half Cheyenne. And the Tewksburys up on Pleasant Valley are half Nez Perce. Bunch of us half-breeds around, you know, and we're all American.'

'That man giving you any trouble, Sam?' The speaker was a shotgun guard on the high chair by the back wall.

I turned to face him. 'You going to toss a law-abiding rancher out of the

Copper King, gunman?' I reached across the bar with my left hand and gripped Sam the bartender's middle finger. I bent it to the breaking point, forcing Sam to hug the bar to try to relieve the pain. 'You fire the sawed-off from where you sit, gunman, and even buckshot will spread far enough to hit Sam. If you don't want to kill the barkeep, don't try killing me. I'm a friendly rancher looking for one lousy drink.'

'Boss!' the shotgunner hollered.

I pulled the Spencer, cocked it, and laid it on the bar.

A door at the back opened and a dandy walked in. His dark-blond hair, parted in the middle and slicked to each side, curled at the collar. His shirt was blinding white and starched stiff as a board. Gray suspenders supported dark grey trousers over mirror-shined wellington boots. 'What is it, Rollins?'

He asked the question, but I could see his eyes taking in the scene and knew that he knew exactly what the situation was.

'That half-breed's trying to buy a drink,' Rollins said. 'He's got Sam so's I can't shoot without hitting him, too.'

'I see. Well . . . ' The man spoke with a funny accent. Sort of like John Tunstall, that Englishman in New Mexico, but sort of different, too. He took half a dozen steps into the room. 'Now see here . . . ' He expected me to supply my name. I said nothing.

'Now see here, Mister . . . ' He paused again, then continued. 'Copper King is a very exclusive saloon, sir, that caters only to gentlemen of breeding. There's no need for you to be violent. It's just that there are certain rules to our business that my employees must obey.'

I looked him in the eye and kept my grip on Sam's finger. 'You the owner?'

'No. I manage the business, add a touch of class, as it were.'

'Because you're English?'

'Welsh.'

I tweaked Sam's finger and he let out

a squeak. 'Maybe you should get the owner out here,' I said.

'One moment.' The Welshman stepped toward the stairway to the second floor.

I tweaked Sam's finger again and picked up the Spencer. 'Don't be sending any shooters from that second story,' I said.

'Of course not.' The Welshman cleared his throat. 'Ahmm. The girls reside on the second floor,' he said. 'I'll inform the owner.'

'You make a funny move and I'll blast you,' Rollins said.

I just smiled.

The Welshman scampered up the stairs. I could hear him tapping on a door. A female voice answered, then the low hum of men talking. A moment later the Welshman came back down. 'The owner will be here directly,' he said.

We all waited, without conversation. A door closed upstairs, and a tall man with no left arm appeared at the landing. I smiled. 'Howdy, Lieutenant,' I said.

The man stopped short. 'Wilder? Sergeant Wilder? Is that you?'

'Rancher Wilder, it is now, sir.'

'What in hell are you doing at the Copper King, Sarge?'

'Trying to buy a shot of rye.'

'You should have sent word.'

'Didn't know you was here.'

'God in Heaven. It's good to see you.' Fitzgerald turned to the Welshman. 'Robert, this is Falan Wilder,' he said. 'He fought off Masai's Apaches the time I lost my arm. Saved my life and those of seven troopers. Earned a Medal of Honor, sort of like your Victoria Cross, I suppose.' Fitzgerald went to sit at a table. 'Bring a bottle of rye, Sam,' he said.

I let go of Sam's finger and holstered the Spencer. The Welshman Robert quietly returned to the back room, and Rollins released the hammers on his sawed-off. The lieutenant poured me a shot of rye. 'On me,' he said.

Sometimes rules get bent.

I took the Cibecue road east from Globe City, dropped into the canyon and crossed Salt River at Horseshoe Bend. Junipers dotted the heights and sycamores bunched along the river. I pointed Zeeb's nose north along Cherry Creek with Lop Ear following meekly behind. There never was a good-natured mule the likes of Lop Ear.

A man doesn't travel without watching his back trail, and I watched mine. No one followed.

Moving along at an easy pace, I reached the mouth of Lone Pine Canyon four days out of Globe City. Me and Zeeb and Lop Ear had climbed steadily since the ford at Horseshoe Bend, so the mouth of Lone Pine was more like a broad meadow with hills on each side. I dug out the remains of the sourdough loaf from King's store and a bit left from a hunk of cheese. The little stream that meandered down Lone

Pine gave me clean, sweet water, and I thought I saw the flickering shadows of native trout. I sat myself crosslegged on the grass and enjoyed a midday meal. Never tasted better.

By sundown I was at the spring that fed the stream, which I'd decided to call Blessing: Blessing Springs, Blessing Creek. Come morning, I'd pace off the boundaries and stake my homestead claim. Nothing around to bother but a robber jay in the piñons, watching to see if I might drop some food.

'Zeb,' I said, 'you keep watch. I'll get some shuteye. You let me know if anything worth looking at comes up the canyon.' I rolled up in the saddle blanket and used the saddle for a pillow. Zeb woke me with a snort while the moon was still high.

'Yudasthir, you are lucky I am not your enemy,' Gosheven said. He sat crosslegged across the dead fire from me.

'My horse said nothing. He knew you for a friend.'

'Hmph. Some friend. One who put holes in your tough hide and spilt your blood in the Circle of the Knife.' Gosheven held his face without expression, mostly. He couldn't keep the mischievous look from his eyes. 'Yudasthir,' he said. 'I have made my vision quest. My totem has spoken.'

'One moment,' I said. 'I am not yet prepared to hear of your vision quest.' I threw off the blanket and made my way to the spring. I removed my shirt and unbuttoned my union suit so I could shrug out of the top and let it hang. I dipped both hands into the cold water and lifted some of it high in my cupped hands, making an offering to *Usen* as my morning sacrifice. I sipped from my hands, swished the water around inside my mouth, then spit it aside from behind the cover of my right hand. I splashed water on my face, my arms, my torso, and dribbled some on my head. I stood still and let the arid air dry my body. I replaced my clothing and returned to the campfire site, ready to listen to Gosheven's odyssey.

In my absence, he'd built a small fire. My little coffee pot sat beside it. 'I don't know where you keep the beans,' he said.

'Later,' I replied. I broke out a bag of Bull Durham. Though I don't like tobacco, it is important to *Usen*. A burning twig from the fire gave me a light for the thick smoke I rolled with paper and tobacco. I filled my mouth with acridness and blew it northward, then toward the south, east, and west. Gosheven did the same.

We sat, the fire between us.

'Yudasthir, you know the ways of *gode*, the spirits that haunt dreams. You will understand when I tell you that my totem was always there. Every time I quested for a vision, my totem was there, ready to speak to me. I expected something fierce, a bear, a wolf, a great eagle, a wily cougar, but my totem is nothing so imposing as they.'

I watched the young man in silence. His eyes told me he'd had a profound experience, something that would shape his life.

He continued. 'Whenever I sought a vision, the same thing happened. As I fasted and prayed, a small bird came. It lit far from me at first, but came closer and closer as it realized I would do it no harm. The bird was always there when I finally broke my fast, and I always gave it a tiny portion of my food.

'This time also, the bird came, seeming to watch me closely with bright black eyes. 'Welcome back, my friend,' I said. It bobbed and moved closer, dressed in dull blacks and browns as is the custom for its kind.

'Late on the second day of my fast, the bird came again. It flitted in from the south and landed on a red sandstone a few feet away. As I watched this common little bird, I heard a voice in my mind: 'You quest for a vision you cannot have,' it said. 'You wish for a fierce one to come and tell you of courage and strife. I say to you, the day for ferocity is past.

''Look at me and learn, young one. Who came to you each time you quested for a vision? A small insignificant bird with no bright feathers, nothing to make it stand out among Earth Mother's children, yet you always shared your food. So it is, young one. The fierce and the proud die young; their blood seeps into the earth. Be like me, young one. Look insignificant. Appear harmless. Have the courage to approach. Have the humility to accept assistance from others. Blend with your surroundings as they change, and you and yours will live long upon the face of Earth Mother. Remember this. Whatever form you appear to take, you are always yourself within.'

'Without waiting for a morsel of my food, the bird flew away.'

Gosheven's shoulders squared and he radiated confidence. 'I am come to learn what you will teach, Wilder. My name is Sparrow.'

He fell silent. Tiny flames ate tentatively at the sticks in the fire. They made tiny pops that sounded loud in the quiet. A bird twittered. Then another. The grey of predawn came. Zeeb and Lop Ear cropped at the lush grass along the stream. Still we sat.

'There is no more,' Sparrow said.

'You learned much,' I said. 'It is enough.' I stood and went to the stack of tools and provisions I'd unloaded from Lop Ear when we reached the spring. I dug for my bag of coffee beans. After crushing a small handful with the butt of the Spencer, I dumped the grounds into the coffee pot. 'We will have coffee soon, Sparrow. You must also take another name. I think one like a Nakai-ye would work well. Pedro, perhaps. Or Ramon. Juan. Raoul. Jaime. Yes. That's a good name. Jaime Sparrow. But we shall always call you Sparrow. It is settled.'

'Jaime Sparrow,' he said, rolling the name on his tongue. 'It tastes well. Thank you, Wilder.'

The sun rose. The sky held no clouds. After a breakfast of sowbelly and saleratus biscuits, it was time to stake my claim to 160 acres at the top end of Long Pine Valley. I strapped the Spencer's gunbelt on. The kukri rode in the small of my back.

Blessing Springs, which fed Blessing Creek, flowed from under the Mogollon Rim. At the spring's source, where it issued from layered sandstone to the edge of the rim, the land climbed at least 500 feet, layers of gray and white, red and brown, rising in a series of flat-topped butte-like hills.

The first levelled off about fifty feet above the spring. A tumble of stones to one side looked like it might be a way up, and I wanted that high place as part of my homestead. I started climbing.

Once I got past the tumbled boulders, a line of footholes went up the rock wall. It wasn't a simple thing to climb the wall, but it wasn't all that hard either, and the way the notches were worn told me many people had used them many times.

When I could see over the lip of the

little plateau, I knew why the foot-holes were worn smooth. I clambered up onto the patch of flat land, and Sparrow, who'd climbed up behind me, followed. He stopped short when he saw the dwelling. 'Hohokam,' he said. 'The ones who went before.'

'Or Anasazi,' I said. 'No way of knowing for sure.'

'We should make a smoke. Spirits may wander this place.'

The dwelling was of sandstone with clay mortar. Three rooms, each about eight by ten. 'No kiva,' I said. 'The dead are not buried here. Those who lived here left this place alive, left it for those who come after.'

'Rider coming,' Sparrow said. 'One man, two horses.'

I looked where he pointed. A small gray pony with a brown packhorse plodded up the trail beside Blessing Creek. 'You stay here,' I said to Sparrow. 'I'll go meet our visitor.'

He said, 'I have no weapon but the Bowie knife.'

I handed him the Spencer. 'It shoots straight for about a hundred paces.'

He nodded. I removed the gunbelt and left that with Sparrow, too.

No shots as I scrambled back down the foot holes in the rock wall. By the time I got back to camp, the horses were swishing through the belly-high grass along the creek. I picked up my Winchester and jacked a cartridge into the chamber.

'Wilder. Wilder.' Blessing rode from behind a copse of scrub oak. 'Will you shoot me then?' she asked.

'My God, but you look good,' I said.

13

The little cliff dwelling above Blessing Springs turned out to be a boon to us. Blessing turned it into a first-rate cabin, and in cleaning the dwelling out, we found pottery shards, disintegrated willow baskets, seashells that had been pierced for stringing, and one turquoise necklace. The fiber that held the stones together had rotted away, but they were all there.

'Some woman from long ago left her treasure for you,' I said to Blessing. She blushed. But from that day on, the turquoise was part of her.

Lone Pine Canyon stretched a dozen miles north and east of where Blessing Creek dumped into the Cherry. It narrowed a bit near the convergence, after cutting through a sandstone rise on its way. My land started at the cut and ranged up the valley. I owned the bottleneck that could protect the ranch and keep stock from wandering away from the upper valley at the same time. Sparrow and I built a sod tool shed and granary not far from Blessing Springs, and Blessing started a vegetable garden. We made a holding pen of cedar poles up against the sandstone wall of the box canyon, and a fence and gate at the place I called Sparrow's Cut.

Zeeb and Lop Ear and Blessing's two horses proceeded to get fat on the good grass that covered the bottom of the valley that was Lone Pine Canyon. With the land I bought and the 160 acres of my homestead, I controlled almost the entire canyon. I figured nearly ten miles from Sparrow's Cut to Blessing Springs, and three miles across at the widest point. At the end of the box canyon, where Blessing Springs gurgled up, there was about a hundred yards from wall to wall.

After buying the land, my stake was getting slim, but on the way to McCullough's place to pick up the horses they held for me, we'd need to get Sparrow some ordinary clothes, a hat, a rifle, and a short gun. Each morning as the sun was struggling up over the Mogollon Rim, Sparrow and I wrestled, boxed, learned Savate kicks, shot the Winchester and the Spencer at likely targets, and raced from Blessing Springs to a big ponderosa about two miles away and back again. The boy was a natural, and after we cut his hair with the Bowie his sharp features looked more Mexican than ever.

Blessing had breakfast ready when we climbed panting to the dwelling after our run. She was an admirable cook. White man's fare of bacon and biscuits was more than OK with me, and Sparrow ate the food like he'd been doing it all his life.

'Sparrow and me will be going up to Aripine to get my horses,' I said. 'I'd appreciate you staying here to look after things.'

Blessing smiled and nodded. 'Never worry,' she said, 'I've got my Yellow Boy and I know how to shoot.'

Never worry, she said, but I should have.

★   ★   ★

The gang was supposed to be waiting for Reed and Bud Fowley at Big Johney Gulch, a town built on the side of a hill that once concealed a rich vein of silver. Now, with the silver long gone, houses stood like toothless corpses and men who couldn't live in ordinary towns staked claims on the empty homes. The Branding Iron opened its doors to all, cash on the barrel head, and Tom Ranklin ruled the town from the second floor.

The Fowleys hitched their horses to the rail and stepped up on the dilapidated boardwalk. 'This place wouldn't last a day in Ehrenburg,' Bud said.

'Don't reckon the people living in this burg got much choice.' Reed hesitated a moment. He took a deep breath. 'Let's go,' he said, and pushed his way into the Branding Iron.

Inside, the saloon looked much better than its gray-slab exterior planking had indicated. A polished bar ran down the left-hand wall, backed by a big mirror with roses etched around its edges. A felt-topped billiards table stood at the end of the room with a faro table next to it. Even the card tables had a well-kept sheen.

A dozen pairs of eyes looked up when the Fowleys barged in. Some returned immediately to their cards or to the whore sitting by their side.

Two pair stayed locked on the Fowleys: the watchman on the high chair and one of the bartenders. Reed strode down the bar to stand in front of the 'keep who kept an eye on the brothers. 'Here to see Tom Ranklin,' he said.

'Lots of folks say that,' the 'keep said.

'Where is he?'

'Oh, here and there. Comes by when he gets a chance.'

'Shit.'

'No need to swear, mister. That's just the way things are. Sit down, have a drink. Mr Ranklin'll be along directly.' The barkeep put two glasses on the bar. 'What'll it be?'

Reed looked at Bud, who shrugged. 'Irish Whiskey,' Reed said.

'What color?'

'Redbreast?'

The bartender shook his head. 'How about Paddy's?'

'That'll do.' Reed Fowley was more than ready for a drink. 'Gimme a bottle.'

The 'keep got a bottle from the hutch and stood it in front of Reed. 'One solid double eagle, that'll be.'

'Jay Zus. Wasn't planning on buying the whole country.'

'Take it or leave it.'

Reed dug a coin from his pocket and plonked it on the bar. 'God damn you to hell,' he said in a pleasant voice.

Reed and Bud Fowley sat at one of the card tables, the bottle of Paddy's whiskey between them. Its level had dropped past the halfway mark. Reed poured more Paddy's into his glass and lifted it with his left hand. He gulped at the whiskey. A rumbling growl started deep in his chest. 'Arrrgh. When we find that 'breed, maybe I won't kill him. Maybe I'll cut the tendons in his heels and see how brave he is when he can't walk.' Reed slugged back the whiskey that remained in his glass. The buzz behind his eyes fed his anger. 'That sumbitch cut me, Bud. He sliced me without so much as a 'by your leave'. This here right arm still don't work right. Sumbitch 'breed. God, I hate that red bastard.'

'Back down, Reed. He ain't no reservation buck,' Bud said. 'You're gonna have to do it right if you want to catch him at all.'

'Sumbitchin' 'breed. I'll get his ass all right, 'n' he'll wish I hadn't.'

'Gentlemen?' A suave man in a white shirt, gray suspenders, and striped California pants walked toward the

Fowleys' table with long, lithe strides. He ran his fingers through his salt-and-pepper hair, which curled slightly around his ears. 'I'm Tom Ranklin. Shotgun Lou Grimes said you wished to engage some men for an expedition into the Tonto Basin. How can I help?'

'Wanna go sumbitchin' 'breed hunting,' Reed said. His voice was too loud and his words slurred together.

'In the Tonto Basin?'

'Yup. Cherry Creek country.'

'Tewksburys?'

'Nope. The bad ass's name'd Falan Wilder.'

Ranklin pulled out a chair. 'May I sit?'

'Help yourself. Your place.' Reed's belligerent side showed through the drink.

Ranklin sat, but stayed stiff and slightly formal. His gray eyes missed little. 'Wilder, you say. Would that be the man who segundoed for Al Sieber at Camp Verde?'

'He was in the Army.'

'Wilder won't come easy,' Ranklin said, 'but I know just the man for this job. Robert Candless. He rode with Chivington against the Cheyenne. Got to be a colonel in the Colorado Volunteers.'

'He here in Big Johney Gulch?'

'He is. I took the liberty of inviting him to meet with us. He'll be down shortly, once he's finished upstairs.'

'We'd surely like to conflab with him.' Bud did the talking now. Reed poured Paddy's and drank it like water, Only a couple of fingers remained in the bottle.

'Candless will want money. And I get a fee for setting you up,' Ranklin said.

'We have money,' Bud said.

Reed nodded, trying to hold his face sober. 'Yeah, we got money,' he said.

'Mind if I see the color?'

Bud pulled out a buckskin poke, opened it, and poured some gold double eagles on the table. 'We've got enough,' he said. 'We'd like to speak to Candless.

Ranklin signalled the barkeep. 'Get Bob Candless from upstairs, and bring these gentlemen another bottle of Paddy's whiskey, on the house.'

'Right, boss,' the 'keep said. 'I'll get right on it.'

Reed broke the seal on a new bottle of Paddy's and poured himself a double shot. He paused, staring at the glass with a look of concentration on his face, shook his head, and put the cork back in the bottle. He mouthed a gulp of whiskey.

A stir at the top of the stairs caught Bud's attention. He poked Reed with an elbow and nodded toward the second floor. Ranklin showed a tiny smile. A tall man in a gray coat with gold-colored piping came down the steps and strode directly to the Fowleys' table.

'Robert Beauregard Candless, at your service,' he said with a stiff bow.

Bud waved at the empty chair. 'Have a seat,' he said.

Candless complied, sitting straight and stiff.

'Drink?' Bud held up the bottle of Paddy's whiskey.

Candless gazed at the bottle for a moment. 'Don't mind if I do,' he said. 'Mind you, I never drink in the field.'

'We hear you rode with Chivington,' Bud said. 'We need to ride down a 'breed who cut my brother.'

'I was a major under Colonel Chivington. Later a colonel in the Colorado Volunteers myself.'

'These men need a light company to go against a former Army scout named Wilder,' Ranklin said. 'I told them you were the man for the job.'

Candless nodded. 'A thousand dollars a week,' he said, 'plus whatever it costs for food and ammunition.'

'When can we ride?' Bud asked.

'I'll want a thousand now and you can pay my quartermaster for provisions and ammo. I'll have a company of riders assembled day after tomorrow morning. Where must we ride to catch this thieving redskin? I assume he will hang. Every red man is good only when dead. I think General Sherman said something to that effect. Astute for a Yankee and a regular Army officer.' Candless took a large drink from his glass. 'Do we have an agreement, then?'

Bud looked at his brother, who was engrossed in pouring more Paddy's into his glass. He pulled a poke from his coat pocket, removed twenty-five gold eagles and shoved the poke across the table toward Candless. 'There's your advance,' he said.

* * *

Candless organized a group of fifteen 'riflemen', a cook and chuck wagon, and a short model .45–70 Gatling gun on a cavalry cart with two horses and two gunners. The preparations took 580 dollars, in addition to the 1,000 dollar advance, from the $9,000 and change that Reed Fowley had when he left Ehrenburg.

'What's the Gatling for?' Bud asked.

'Raferty used Gatlings to advantage

against Black Horse and his Sioux,' Candless said. He rode a dapple gray that could have been sired by General Lee's Traveler.

The men lined up in two rows, just like cavalry, the Gatling at the left, the chuck wagon behind. Candless paraded his gray horse in front of them. 'We have been commissioned to ride against the barbaric red man,' he shouted. 'By line of twos, forwa-a-rd, ho-o-o-o.'

Bud and Reed rode just behind Candless. Reed's head hung and bobbed with his horse's pace as he suffered the effects of Paddy's whiskey.

The cavalcade travelled twenty miles a day, keeping the horses at a walk. 'It's better the men enter a conflict fresh,' Candless said. 'We've oats to keep the horses fit, too.'

Reed had brought two bottles of Paddy's whiskey, which were long gone by the end of the third day. He suffered another two days without whiskey until the company reached Pleasant Valley at the headwaters of Cherry Creek. They camped two miles from Mormon Farm in a meadow lined with ponderosa pines. A small stream supplied water.

Once the men were bivouacked, Candless came to the Fowleys on his dapple gray. 'I'll ride to Mormon Farm,' he said. 'Lot Smith usually knows what's going on in this territory. Will you come along?'

'I'll go,' Bud said. 'Give me a minute to saddle up.'

Reed lay motionless on the grass, his head on his saddle, hat over his eyes.

'I'll check the Gatling, then. You can meet me there when you are ready.' Candless spurred the gray into a gallop, and its iron-shod hoofs threw clods, which almost hit Reed.

'Sumbitch,' Reed said. 'Uppity bastard. Who in Hell does he think is paying him?'

Bud said nothing. He merely saddled his horse and got ready to ride to Mormon Farm. Then, holding the reins to his bay, he said, 'Reed. For a man nursing a grudge, you're showing piss-poor judgement. From what I seen of Wilder, he'd eat you alive. I figure it's time you started acting like a man instead of a half-grown kid. I'm going with Candless to find out what the Mormon Smith knows. You pull yourself together.' Bud mounted and spurred the bay after Candless.

After Bud left, Reed Fowley lay staring at the sky. He was almighty thirsty for whiskey. A single pull on a bottle would settle his stomach and soothe the fever in his brain. He knew it would. The triangle announcing dinner clanged. Reed lifted his head to watch the riflemen and Gatling crew drift over to the cook fire. He wasn't hungry, but maybe Cookie had a bottle stashed away for emergencies. Reed stirred, then got to his feet and walked slowly to the chuck wagon, hoping against hope.

The cook dished up beans and fried beef to the men, keeping up a constant banter. Reed waited in the shadows behind the wagon.

The cook came back to the wagon for more salt. 'Hsst.' Reed hissed to catch the his attention. 'Cookie.'

'Evenin', Mr Fowley,' the cook said in his normal loud gravelly voice.

'I was wondering,' Reed said, licking his lips. 'Might you have a supply of medicinal spirits in this wagon?'

'You mean whiskey?'

Reed glanced about, then nodded.

'I might have some.'

'Not feeling too well, and thought a shot or two might help.' Reed's face took on a hopeful expression.

'I reckon I could give you a dram,' the cook said.

'If it's all the same to you, I'd like to buy one of your bottles. Save having to come back if my complaint don't clear up. Would ten dollars cover it?' Reed held out a gold eagle.

The cook grinned. 'I reckon,' he said, and plucked the coin from Reed's hand.

When Bud got back from Mormon Farm with news that someone had settled in Lone Pine Canyon, the bottle was empty and Reed lay spreadeagled, snoring. Bud heaved a sigh. His little brother became more of a burden each day, but the quest for Falan Wilder would soon be over and he could take Reed back to Ehrenburg. After that, Reed would be on his own.

Next day, the company moved carefully through Sparrow's Cut into the meadows of Lone Pine. The riflemen tore Wilder's split rail fence apart and shattered the plank over the gate that was branded with a Flying W. They bivouacked up the canyon about five miles. As the cook fire burned in the Candless camp and the sun hovered on the edge of Black Mesa, Blessing sent up a smoke.

14

The McCulloughs had treated my horses right. The stallion was a youngster, just three years old, and the spitting image of Big Red. He'd throw strong colts, and I called him Little Red. I'd picked the mares from all the mustangs we'd caught last summer. Three were long-legged and short-coupled, built for speed. Two were broad in the shoulders and across the hips. They looked to have more than a little Morgan blood, and that was no disadvantage. The rest were good solid stock but not showy.

'We kept the mares separated from the stud,' Kimberly McCullough said. 'Didn't think you'd want to be tending colts right off.' She rode a little black filly with white stockings that might as well have been greased lightning. The kid called the horse Big

222

Enough, and she surely was.

'Wouldn't want to sell me that tiny black filly, would you?' I had to try.

She grinned. 'Don't you wish. You know Big Enough took the big race in Holbrook last year, going away.' The kid's chest swelled with pride in her fast horse.

'Anyone spoke for first colt?'

She nodded. 'Russ Taklin,' she said, and blushed.

'Second?'

A shake of her head. 'Nope.'

'I dibs first filly,' I said. 'Unless it's the first foal. Then I'll take second filly, no questions asked.'

'Done,' she said.

Sparrow couldn't take his eyes off the kid, and comely she was. Dark from her Mexican mother, thin-faced and hawk-nosed from her pa.

'If you'll let us sleep in your barn, we'll be heading out for Cherry Creek country at dawn,' I said.

'Help yourself. Kane and Kenigan and Pa'll be back by dusk, I reckon. You can jaw with them before you go.'

We corralled the horses and fed them, rubbed down Zeeb and Blessing's little gray, which Sparrow rode. Lop Ear and the packhorse stayed at the Flying W. We took our saddles and blankets and made nests for ourselves in the hayloft. There's nothing more relaxing than sleeping on fresh hay.

The evening meal at McCullough's place was tasty venison stew, and it felt good to eat at a bona fide table. We shot the bull while the old man and Kane smoked their pipes. The Apaches came not long after we climbed into the loft for the night.

A light showed at the big double door. 'Wilder?' Kane McCullough's voice came from below.

'I'm here, Kane,' I said. Sparrow slipped to the edge of the loft, squatting in a corner where he seemed to fade into the woodwork.

'Man here to see you,' Kane said.

I pulled on my boots, shoved the Spencer behind my waistband, and backed my way down the ladder. The new moon was up, so Kane doused the lantern as soon as I got down. 'Come with me, Wilder,' he said, setting the lantern on a shelf just inside the door.

We walked across the clearing around the house and barn toward a grove of jack pines on the southeast edge. As we neared, a shadow stepped from among the trees. 'Yudasthir,' a voice said. 'I am Alchesay.'

I greeted the Apache and waited for him to speak.

'We know not what has happened,' he said, 'but the woman sent up a smoke from your rancheria in the evening one day ago.'

My heart dropped with a thud I could almost hear. My mouth went dry. I hardly managed to speak. 'Kane,' I said. 'I'll have to leave my horses with you a little longer. I'll ride my Zeeb and lead Little Red. Sparrow can take the gray he came on and the chestnut mare. We'll be riding hard.'

Sparrow and Alchesay moved back

into the pines. I could hear snatches of their conversation, but wasn't paying attention. I thought only of Blessing. I'd left her alone and now she was in trouble. We had to ride, and ride fast.

'Kane, we'll be riding into trouble. If you've got any extra .44–40 cartridges, I'd like to buy them from you.'

'You can have what we've got, Wilder, but I reckon it'll be only a couple of boxes or so.'

'Lots better than going into a fight with what I've got in my belt.'

Kane went for the ammunition while Sparrow and I saddled our horses. 'Alchesay will make smoke,' Sparrow said.

'Best the Apaches stay out of this,' I said. 'Things could get nasty if they're involved.'

Sparrow said nothing.

Kane returned with three boxes of shells and a small bag of loose cartridges. 'Take it, Wilder. We'll get more in Round Valley.'

'If you're going in that direction,

could you drop by the RP Connected and tell Marshal Havelock there'll probably be shooting trouble at Lone Pine Canyon?'

'I'll do it,' Kane said.

We rode hard, and we rode straight, passing north of Wolf Mountain and taking the plateau past Adair on to Phoenix Park in the ponderosa pine belt above the rim. From Phoenix Park, we turned west toward the edge of the Mogollon Rim, which stood above and somewhat north and east of Lone Pine Canyon. We found a way off the rim and onto a flat-topped hill that let us see into Lone Pine Canyon. We slithered up to the edge to see what was going on below. We'd abandoned our white man's hats for dirty brown headbands with sticks and leaves stuck in them. Nothing draws the eye like an unnatural shape — a big hat, for instance.

Smoke from a dozen fires rose and flattened out when it hit the breeze sweeping off the rim. I counted twenty-two horses in a rope corral on the south side of Blessing Creek. Lop Ear and the packhorse were in the corral. A bunch of men were gathered around the fire by a chuck wagon. A tent stood a few yards away with another fire smoldering in front of it. I was too far away to recognize anyone.

I fumbled for the field glasses I always carried and brought them to my eyes. The glasses brought the men below close enough for me to read their faces. Three I knew. One was Reed Fowley, the man I'd cut with my Bowie in Ehrenburg. I felt for the kukri nestled in the small of my back. The second was Reed's brother Bud. He didn't look happy. The third was a face I'd not seen in nearly twenty years. It was a face I'd not likely forget, though I couldn't put a name to it. When Chivington's men killed the women and children at Sand Creek, that face was behind the gun that shot my own mother. I made a vow. That man would not leave Lone Pine Canyon alive.

Then the glasses showed me another reason that man had to die. A post stood on the far side of the tent. The hounds who called themselves men had tied Blessing to the post, wrists lashed together and fastened high above her head. She was naked, and I could see the Fowleys and their men had not been kind to her. As I watched, Reed Fowley upended a bottle and took a long swig from it. He said something and the man from Sand Creek laughed. Bud got a pained look on his face. Reed took another swig and walked toward Blessing, fumbling at his britches. A couple of feet from her, he got his pecker out of his pants and started pissing on Blessing, up and down her body, and then a splash on her face. Her eyes glittered. Reed stuck his face up close to hers and said something. Blessing spit in his eyes, and he smashed her face with an open hand, then back-handed her with a half-closed fist. Blood dribbled from the corner of her mouth, but the glitter never left her eyes, nor did she cry out.

Reed Fowley had just signed his death warrant.

I handed the glasses to Sparrow and signed for him to look. A glance at the scene below was enough. He gave the glasses back. *That man must die*, I signed.

Slowly, Sparrow signed back.

Soon night would fall, and in the darkness the men who had invaded my Flying W ranch would begin to die, for a man has a right to defend and protect what is his.

We backed away from the rim and picketed the horses. They'd make out on the grama, though it was sparse, and the way to the canyon floor was easier for a man.

Sparrow and I held a quiet war council. 'The men are hired,' I said. 'Kill only to protect yourself. But two of the men must die. The tall one with white hair under his hat, for he is the man who killed my mother in a place called Sand Creek. The thick man who struck Blessing must also die . . . and his brother with him if it comes to that.'

Sparrow's eyes narrowed. 'I take only the knife I received from Yudasthir, and the skills taught me by the man called Wilder,' he said.

'Leave no sign that says Apache,' I said. 'If it looks like Apaches killed white men, the innocent among your people will suffer.'

'I understand,' Sparrow said.

'First, find the men who stand watch,' I said. 'You are a barred owl. I am a nightjar. Call once when a man is down and out of the fight. Call twice if you need me to come to you. I will do the same.' I pocketed three leather thongs and tied a piggin string about my waist. I handed some thongs and another piggin string to Sparrow. I tucked the Spencer behind my waistband.

We waited for the night to deepen. The fires below winked out one by one,

231

except for the cook fire by the chuck wagon. 'You take the south rim,' I said to Sparrow, 'I will move along the north one. We go.'

I slipped over the edge of our little plateau into a steep gully that wound its way to the canyon floor. Both Sparrow and I wore knee-high moccasins and most of our clothing blended well with the varicolored sandstone and patches of scrub oak and Utah juniper that line the edges of the canyon. As I neared the bottom I caught a whiff of wood smoke tinged with tobacco. I froze. Slowly I searched the area before me, dividing it into sections and turning only a tiny bit each time I needed to adjust my field of view.

A faint red glow. The lookout on my side of the creek sealed his fate with hunger for a smoke. Ordinary night sounds lulled the guard, I reckon. The click of beetles, the soft chortling of mourning doves, the rough clicking cry of nightjars. I crept toward the lookout.

'Hey, Buck.' The call came from

across Blessing Creek. The lookout stirred. 'Black as the insides of a grizzly,' the voice said. 'What in hell are we supposed to see out here. Shit.'

'Shut up.' My lookout spoke low with a sharp edge to his voice that carried.

I crouched not three feet away. The lookout ground the remains of his smoke under his heel and I smashed the barrel of my Spencer against the side of his head. He went down, but came right back up. His elbow took me in the jaw and brought bright specks before my eyes.

'Enemy!' the lookout hollered.

So much for silence. I managed to ear back the Spencer's hammer and pull the trigger a second before the lookout got his gun into play. The bullet took him in the throat. I left him choking on his own blood.

The hoot of a barred owl told me Sparrow had taken care of the lookout on his side. I made the grating sound of a nightjar's call.

'Buck! Sam! What is it? Who is it?'

I faded back into the cedars, taking the lookout's rifle with me. Darkness was still my friend.

As I slipped toward the camp through the willows along the creek bank, dark shapes and pounding boots told me men were coming to the lookouts' aid, too late.

'Buck's dead!'

'Sam, too.'

'Spread out. Find the bastards.'

Nearer the camp, I could see someone had built up the fire. It cast a ring of light on the surrounds. Lying on my stomach in the willows, I took stock of what was going on.

Blessing had her head up. She must have been hurting, but she didn't show it. Then I saw the Gatling gun. The time for stealth was over. I made the nightjar call twice, and started for the wash that led to the plateau where we'd left the horses and my one-in-a-thousand Winchester.

Shouts still sounded in the night as I topped out on the little plateau.

Sparrow wasn't there. With my Winchester in hand, I bellied up to the rim. I picked a spot between two boulders that would give me cover if I needed it. A short Gatling gun, .45 caliber. The Fowleys hadn't come for a fight, they were planning a massacre.

Only one fire burned bright. The others hadn't been restarted. I picked a dim form, lined up the Winchester's sights, and finessed the trigger. To me, the roar of the rifle was loud and strong, but in camp it would be a pop.

The bullet struck the man before the sound could reach the camp. He quivered and lay still. Someone shouted.

I held my fire.

Two men ran to the Gatling and swung it around. My rifle put one down, but didn't kill him. He howled and screeched. Any Cheyenne would be ashamed of the noise he made.

I held my fire.

The tall man in the gray coat strode from the tent. He must have taken time to dress properly. He cupped his hands around his mouth and shouted. A moment later, I heard, 'Riflemen. To me!'

One shot from my one-in-a-thousand Winchester would put him down, but I wanted to look in his eyes when he died. I held my fire.

Bud Fowley came from the tent. There was no sign of Reed.

Men gathered in front of the tent. I counted fourteen plus the cook, so we faced seventeen or eighteen guns. For the moment, they seemed to have forgotten Blessing.

The tall man shouted and gestured, and two men ran for the Gatling, where the wounded man still writhed. As they bent over him I lined my sights on the gun's magazine and touched off the trigger. My bullet spanged off the breech, hitting it just forward of the upright magazine and ricocheting into the magazine itself. With luck, the Gatling was out of commission. The two men flattened out, hiding behind the wounded man. I switched my attention to the main group, picked the rifleman closest to Blessing and put a bullet through his head. The riflemen scattered. The tall man and Bud Fowley took cover behind the chuck wagon.

The sky grayed as dawn threatened.

A man lay sprawled on the far side of where Blessing stood tied to the post. I didn't remember shooting him. Bullets chipped at the boulders that sheltered me, then I heard the rifles pop. I slipped around the far side of one of the boulders and edged my Winchester out to where I could aim and shoot. The man near Blessing was closer, and sprawled in a different position. Sparrow!

I stood up behind my boulder and fed cartridges into my rifle, then stepped out into the open. From more than 400 yards away and shooting uphill, wasn't one man in a hundred who'd hit what he aimed at. I shot and levered and shot and levered as fast as I could work the rifle's action. My bullets started with the men closest to Blessing

237

and worked out from there. The third shot had them huddling behind cover. One more man was down. The fourth shot saw Sparrow leap to the post and cut Blessing loose with a single swipe of his Bowie. Rather than take the time to cut her bonds, he just threw her over his shoulder and disappeared into the brush.

My Winchester was empty. I dropped back behind the boulder and started feeding bullets into the magazine. None of the shots fired by the Fowleys' riflemen had come close . . . well, none had hit me, though rock chips had nicked my face.

Day had come, and it was a good day to die, if it came to that.

15

The Gatling gun chattered and its .45 caliber bullets started chewing on the sandstone that protected me. My shot had not disabled the gun after all. I cowered behind the big boulders.

The riflemen would be trying to get me under the cover of the Gatling's hail of lead. I grabbed the sack of bullets Kane McCullough had given me, dumped another boxful into it, pulled the Spencer and checked its loads, patted the kukri in the small of my back, and crabbed my way across the little plateau toward the wash that led to the floor of Lone Pine Canyon. Under my breath, I started singing my death song: *Eiya eiya haiya ha ho yey eiya haiya yaiya hoyey eiya hoya hey . . .*

At the bottom of the wash, I took time to hang the bag of bullets from my neck so I could just reach in and grab new cartridges. I stepped out of the scrub and started walking across the meadow toward the chuck wagon and the tent. I sang my death song, but no one could hear it above the thunder of the Gatling.

The riflemen labored up the steep incline toward the rim. The tall man stood by the chuck wagon, saber in hand, shouting at the men. I brought my one-in-a-thousand to my shoulder and shot the man who fed magazines into the Gatling. He fell away. I shot the Gatling's gunner. The gun fell silent.

'He's only one man, you bastards.' The tall man's shout sounded loud in the stillness.

Eiya eiya haiya ha ho yey eiya haiya yaiya hoyey eiya hoya hey . . . . I drew bead on the tall man and shot him through the thigh, back to front. He tumbled, clutching at the wound. I shifted the Winchester toward the riflemen. I fired as quickly as I could lever shells into the chamber. Some of my bullets hit home. More missed. I sang. The riflemen shot back. A bullet clipped off part of my ear and blood ran down the side of my neck. Two more men went down under my Winchester.

Another voice joined my song and Sparrow strode from the scrub oak cover and came to stand beside me. He held a rifle, probably from one of the dead. He bled from a wound under his left arm, but it didn't affect his shooting. Our practice paid off. We sang. I pushed more bullets into my Winchester. Sparrow fired with care. Another man went down. I wondered where the Fowleys were.

A sound like a bugle came from far down the canyon. I fired, then fired again. A man stood from behind a bush, his arms flung wide. He toppled. I jacked the lever and squeezed off a shot at the crown of a hat I saw sticking up from behind an old log. The hat spun away. I didn't know if I'd hit its owner. The bugle sounded closer now. I sang.

I shot a glance over my shoulder. A

line of horsemen clad in blue cantered up the meadow. A man in dark gray rode on the outside. I caught the glint of a badge on his chest. On command, the horsemen fired a volley from their Springfields. The bullets whapped overhead.

'Cease fire,' bellowed a voice I'd heard give commands before. 'Lay down your weapons, all of you.'

Carefully, I laid my Winchester on the ground. Sparrow looked at me, a question in his eyes. I nodded. He laid his rifle down, too. I shucked the Spencer and placed it beside the Winchester.

One by one, the hired riflemen stood up, their hands empty. There were only nine.

Bud Fowley crawled from under the chuck wagon, his hands at shoulder height. Still no sign of Reed.

'Major,' I called.

'What is it, Sergeant?'

'There's a lady in the scrub without no clothes. I'm going to walk over and give her my shirt.' I started undoing the buttons.

'Go.'

I found Blessing sitting on a rock behind a screen of live oak. Before I could shrug out of my shirt, she jumped up, ran to me, and threw her arms around my waist. 'I thought they'd kill you,' she said, her voice trembling.

'Not that easy to kill,' I said. 'Did they hurt you? Do anything to you?'

She nodded. 'Hurt. Did. But I'm here.'

I felt her grasp the handle of the kukri and pull it from its sheath. 'I'll borrow this,' she said. 'Give me the shirt.'

I did.

While I'm not a big man, my shirt still came to mid-thigh on Blessing.

'Let's go,' she said, and tucked her left hand in the crook of my right elbow. Ordinarily, I'd have her on my left side to keep my right hand free, but Major Simmons would have the rabble under control, so I let it be.

The riflemen were bunched up near the chuck wagon with a half circle of troopers holding Springfields on them. The tall man sat with his back against a chuck wagon wheel, a tourniquet on his leg, and the Fowleys stood off to one side, their faces downcast.

I'd seen one badge, but there were two. The man in gray I knew; the one in the black leather vest I didn't. Blessing held the kukri against the back of her right leg as we walked toward the men. Sparrow stepped up alongside her.

On the way by I picked up my Winchester and shoved the Spencer behind my waistband. Sparrow retrieved the rifle he'd laid down. Blessing kept me between her and Major Simmons. Her right hand was out of sight.

The Fowleys seemed to want to steer shy of the tall man. Ness Havelock, the man in gray, spoke. 'I reckon you all know it's breaking the law to destroy another man's property. But it's not a federal crime, so you're out of my jurisdiction. That's why Sheriff

Bozworth is here.' Havelock nodded at the man with the black leather vest. 'The sheriff takes care of state crimes.'

'It is no crime to remonstrate filthy redskins.' The tall man spit out the words, froth flying from his mouth. Then I learned his name.

'Robert Candless,' the major said. 'I know you rode with that killer Chivington. I know you were once a colonel with the Colorado Volunteers. I also know you rob trains and hold up Wells Fargo. I reckon Marshal Havelock will take custody of you.'

I drew the Spencer, stalked over to Candless, and shoved the muzzle against his head.

'Wilder!' The major barked my name.

I didn't move. 'So your name is Candless, then?' I raised my voice. 'Major, I was a kid of eleven summers when Chivington hit our village at Sand Creek, but I was old enough to remember this man. My mother was on her hands and knees, trying to find some protection when this man rode up on a fine bay horse and shot her dead. I swore to take his life for hers.' I cocked the Spencer.

'Hold it, Wilder,' Havelock said. 'By rights, Candless should die, but I've got to ask you to let me do it. If we're ever to get rid of the fighting and feuding, it's got to be with the law. Let me do it, Falan Wilder. I promise your mother will rest easy when the law is finished with this poor excuse for a man.'

I dearly wanted to pull the trigger. No one spoke. I took a deep breath and held it. My hand trembled, banging the barrel of the Spencer against Candless's head. I let the breath out and released the Spencer's hammer. 'He's yours, Marshal,' I said, and backed away. I shoved the Spencer back behind my waistband.

'If that's all . . . ' The major turned toward the troopers.

'It's not all,' Blessing said. She marched over to Reed Fowley, the tail of my shirt flapping in the slight breeze, and me standing there in my union suit.

Reed just looked at her, a smirk on his face. Blessing stepped closer. She barely came up to his shoulder. 'After what you done,' she said, 'I oughta kill you. But dying's too good for your kind.' She reached up with her left hand and grabbed his nose. At the same time, her right hand brought my kukri swinging out and around, and she sliced through Reed's nose just behind her fingers. The blade cut flesh and cartilage like it was cutting cake, and Blessing stepped back with the end of Reed Fowley's nose in her hand.

For a split second Reed didn't know what had happened. By reflex, his hand jumped up to cover his nose. Blood dribbled down his chin, but the severed stump bled little, considering. Reed screamed.

No one moved.

Blessing held up the end of Reed's nose. 'Now people will see you for the man you are,' she said. She wiped the kukri on my shirt and handed it to me.

She turned to Major Simmons. 'That's all,' she said.

★ ★ ★

Jaime Sparrow came thundering up the canyon, smacking his long-legged black lightly with his quirt to get an extra spurt of speed. 'Riders coming,' he hollered. 'One of 'em is Marshal Havelock.' Sparrow's English was good as any cowpoke's now.

Blessing opened the door to our Texas-style cabin and stepped out . . . well, waddled out, her being heavy with child.

Sparrow jumped off the black and come to stand by my side. Our other hand, a man named Montana, rode up and joined us. We waited for the riders to arrive.

They came up the canyon four abreast. Ness Havelock rode on the outside, and before long I recognized Sean Fowley and Sergeant-Major Darragh Regan, in uniform. I'd never seen

248

the fourth man before, but his resemblance to the sergeant-major made me figure he was Dutch.

'G'day, Wilder,' Havelock said as the four riders reined in. 'Mind if we get down?'

I looked at the sergeant-major. He smiled and nodded. Sean Fowley didn't look at me at all.

'Light and sit,' I said, waving at the benches in the dog run. 'Coffee?'

'Coffee would hit the spot,' Havelock said. The four men dismounted.

'Good to see you, Falan,' the sergeant-major said. 'This is Dutch.' He put a hand on the younger man's arm. I nodded.

I brought two chairs from the cabin and put them in the shade of the dog run, the roofed area between the cabin and the bunkhouse. Havelock and Dutch sat on the bench against the cabin wall, Regan and Fowley took the one against the bunkhouse. Sparrow and I sat on the chairs. The smell of coffee wafted from the cabin. Then

Blessing came with a coffee pot and tin cups. Sparrow jumped to take the coffee pot while Blessing gave everyone a cup. She took the pot and poured the coffee, then went back into the cabin. We sipped at the hot brew, except for Sean Fowley.

After what felt like a long silence, Fowley spoke. 'Falan Wilder,' he said, 'I've come with my friend Darragh Regan to make peace.' He sucked in a deep breath. The lines in his face seemed to deepen. 'I came to this country as a young man. The potatoes failed in Eire, they did, and we came hungry and hoping for something better than we had in the old country. Shunned, we were, but Irishmen banded together, trusted each other, and fought to build a place for us in this land.'

I had no idea where he was going, but Fowley was a guest at my house and I owed him the courtesy of listening. I caught a glimpse of Blessing's gingham dress near the open window. Little Red bugled at his mares from across Blessing Creek.

'We could na take insult or injury lightly,' Fowley said. 'If we got hit, we hit back harder, ya see. I fought in the war with Darragh Regan in the Irish Brigade, the Fighting 69th. He saved me life more than once. He stayed in the Army, as ye know. I took to the railroad, working the rail gangs, setting up whiskey for the men, and providing their women.' A cough racked Fowley and he spat phlegm into a handkerchief. I thought I saw blood. He lifted his head to look me in the eye for the first time.

'I tried to raise me sons right, and it went well until Meaghan, my wife, she died.' Fowley stared at the toes of his boots for a minute or two.

'I tried,' he said again, 'but now my boys are in jail. I'm not blaming you, Wilder. I knew Reed had a mean streak. The night he gambled away the Black Diamond, before he set out to kill you, he beat a whore named Polly. She died.'

'Polly?'

He nodded. 'The woman at Adam's Well.'

'Shit.' I heard a sniffle from the cabin.

Fowley went on. 'But now he's in the hell-hole at Yuma, paying his dues. Bud got a year for his part. He just came home, he did.'

No one spoke for a time. The coffee cups were nearly empty. A horse stomped, and the milk-cow lowed for her calf.

'Falan Wilder,' Fowley said. 'Us Fowleys used you hard, did to you what you never deserved. Darragh Regan told me of you, he did, and I'm begging your pardon. Could you let bygones go?'

I fasten Fowley with a hard eye. 'Sean Fowley, all I ever wanted from you and yours was a drink for the road. I'm a 'breed. Some folks think we got no rights, but we do. Same as you. Now, you're a guest at the Flying W. You're welcome whenever you come, just like any neighbor. Lots of people take new names when they come west. Darragh Regan gave me mine. I'm proud of that name. Sergeant Major Regan is your friend, and he's given me more than I can ever pay back. So . . . yes. Bygones are bygones. Some day, I'll be in Ehrenburg, and I'll come by for a drink.'

Fowley nodded. 'My thanks, Falan Wilder. The doors of the Shamrock are always open to ye.'

'Wilder?' Ness Havelock spoke. 'Some of the men who came after you had rewards on their heads.' He handed me a bank draft for $375.

'I never caught no one,' I said.

'They tore up your place. Maybe this'll help. No one else claimed it.'

I put the draft in my shirt pocket and nodded my thanks.

'Candless went to Leavenworth prison. He got fifteen years,' Havelock said.

'Ain't enough.'

'Leave it be, Wilder.' Havelock turned to the others. 'We'd better ride. Globe

City's some ways away.'

Montana brought their horses.

'Ye've done well,' the sergeant-major said. 'I'm proud of ye.'

Dutch stuck out a hand. I took it. 'Glad to meet the man who stood off half the Apache nation and saved my pa's neck,' he said, 'and I thank you.' He paused a moment. Blessing came out of the cabin to stand with me. 'Mind if I stop by when I'm in the area?' Dutch asked.

'The brother of my husband is always welcome at our fire,' Blessing said.

Ness Havelock raised a finger to his hat. 'Keep your eyes peeled, 'breed,' he said.

I laughed. 'You, too, 'breed,' I said.

'It's over,' Blessing said as the four men rode away.

'Yes,' I said, 'it's over.' I turned to Montana and Sparrow. 'Don't just stand there gawking. We got work to do.'

The stallion bugled again.

We do hope that you have enjoyed reading this large print book.

Did you know that all of our titles are available for purchase?

We publish a wide range of high quality large print books including:
Romances, Mysteries, Classics
General Fiction
Non Fiction and Westerns

Special interest titles available in large print are:
The Little Oxford Dictionary
Music Book, Song Book
Hymn Book, Service Book

Also available from us courtesy of Oxford University Press:
Young Readers' Dictionary
(large print edition)
Young Readers' Thesaurus
(large print edition)

For further information or a free brochure, please contact us at:
Ulverscroft Large Print Books Ltd.,
The Green, Bradgate Road, Anstey,
Leicester, LE7 7FU, England.
Tel: (00 44) **0116 236 4325**
Fax: (00 44) **0116 234 0205**

CUT-PRICE LAWMAN

Tyler Hatch

They wanted a sheriff they could control and run the town their way . . . then along came Chris Cade: a drifter, drunk, stupid with toothache and broke. The badge was easy to pin on him. But Cade, with his own agenda and rules, had a pair of hard fists and a fast gun. They figured they'd got him for a cut-rate, but the price they paid put them deep in the red — and the well-turned soil of Boot Hill.